Books by Janet Lambert

PENNY PARRISH STORIES
Star Spangled Summer 1941
Dreams of Glory 1942
Glory Be! 1943
Up Goes the Curtain 1946
Practically Perfect 1947
The Reluctant Heart 1950

TIPPY PARRISH STORIES
Miss Tippy 1948
Little Miss Atlas 1949
Miss America 1951
Don't Cry Little Girl 1952
Rainbow After Rain 1953
Welcome Home, Mrs. Jordan 1953
Song in Their Hearts 1956
Here's Marny 1969

JORDAN STORIES
Just Jenifer 1945
Friday's Child 1947
Confusion by Cupid 1950
A Dream for Susan 1954
Love Taps Gently 1955
Myself & I 1957
The Stars Hang High 1960
Wedding Bells 1961
A Bright Tomorrow 1965

PARRI MACDONALD STORIES
Introducing Parri 1962
That's My Girl 1964
Stagestruck Parri 1966
My Davy 1968

CANDY KANE STORIES
Candy Kane 1943
Whoa, Matilda 1944
One for the Money 1946

DRIA MEREDITH STORIES
Star Dream 1951
Summer for Seven 1952
High Hurdles 1955

CAMPBELL STORIES
The Precious Days 1957
For Each Other 1959
Forever and Ever 1961
Five's a Crowd 1963
First of All 1966
The Odd Ones 1969

SUGAR BRADLEY STORIES
Sweet as Sugar 1967
Hi, Neighbor 1968

CHRISTIE DRAYTON STORIES
Where the Heart Is 1948
Treasure Trouble 1949

PATTY AND GINGER STORIES
We're Going Steady 1958
Boy Wanted 1959
Spring Fever 1960
Summer Madness 1962
Extra Special 1963
On Her Own 1964

CINDA HOLLISTER STORIES
Cinda 1954
Fly Away Cinda 1956
Big Deal 1958
Triple Trouble 1965
Love to Spare 1967

DON'T CRY, LITTLE GIRL

Dear Readers:

Mother always said she wanted her books to be good enough to be found in someone's attic!

After all of these years, I find her stories—not in attics at all—but prominent in fans' bookcases just as mine are. It is so heart-warming to know that through these republications she will go on telling good stories and being there for her "girls," some of whom find no other place to turn.

With a heart full of love and pride–
Janet Lambert's daughter,
Jeanne Ann Vanderhoef

DON'T CRY, LITTLE GIRL

By

Janet Lambert

Image Cascade Publishing

First *Image Cascade Publishing* edition published 2000.
Copyright renewed © 1980 by Jeanne Ann Vanderhoef

Library of Congress Cataloging in Publication Data
Lambert, Janet 1895-1973
    Don't cry, little girl.

(Juvenile Girls)
Reprint. Originally published: New York: E. P.
Dutton, 1952.

ISBN 1-930009-21-6 (Pbk.)

For Billie

DON'T CRY, LITTLE GIRL

There! little girl, don't cry!
  They have broken your heart, I know;
  And the rainbow gleams
  Of your youthful dreams
  Are things of the long ago:
    But Heaven holds all for which you sigh.—
    There! little girl, don't cry!

(By Permission of The Bobbs-Merrill Company, Inc.
  From the book, *Afterwhiles*.)

CHAPTER I

T𝚒𝚙𝚙𝚢 P𝚊𝚛𝚛𝚒𝚜𝚑 sat on the front seat of the family car and wondered why the first Congress of the United States had felt it necessary to move its capital city from New York to Washington. Left where it was, she could have driven down from her home in the country in her customary, and leisurely, hour and a half. This way, it seemed the longest drive she had ever endured, for other cars and trucks were on the road to Washington, too, and her father was such a careful driver. "Honestly, Dad," she exclaimed at last, "if you don't try to pass that old goat ahead of you, we'll *never* get there!"

"Have patience," Colonel Parrish answered, unperturbed and watching the ancient car and driver that wabbled back and forth across the white dividing line. "I'd rather arrive late and in one piece then pile up somewhere. Besides, this young man of yours won't even fly in until sometime tomorrow. You might just as well be moving along with something to watch as sit in a hotel room, your eyes on a clock."

"Maybe." Tippy sighed and sat back. She saw the good sense in his remark; but, since she was on her way to meet a very special young officer who was coming home from Germany for only a few days before he went on to Korea, she bounced up again to ask, "What if that busy old general won't give Ken enough time off to do things with me?"

11

"I wouldn't worry about that—yet. Just wait and let things work out."

Colonel Parrish looked down at the small, tense face beside him. Tippy was the youngest of his four children, and the most serious. Her hazel eyes were always golden mirrors for her reflections, either gay or somber, and little dimples at the corners of her upturned lips winked when she laughed, even when she cried, in a heart-touching way that was childish and sweet. She had always been his little golden girl, with golden curls to match her eyes, and he wished she could have stayed that way and not grown up and fallen in love. "I should have put a brick on your head," he said, expressing his thoughts aloud, "like you asked me to do when you were five"; and she leaned back again and laughed.

"You wouldn't like having a dwarfed moron to lead around," she retorted. "And I suppose *you* never grew up and fell in love with Mums and wanted to get married!"

"Not till I was a respectable age. I didn't even know girls existed at eighteen."

"Ha-ha." A hollow laugh came from the back seat and turned Tippy around. Mrs. Parrish had ensconced herself there for a nap but her brown eyes were wide open and twinkling. "Don't believe him," she said, yawning. "He tortured me when I was seven years old."

"But I didn't love you. I simply endured you because your parents happened to live in the same block with mine."

The slowpoke was at last behind them and Colonel Parrish settled down in his seat for a sprint that might be long or short, dependent on traffic ahead. His children all knew he had spent four long years as a cadet in West Point, suffering agony lest someone older, well established and ready to marry, should lure the girl from home away from him. They knew, too, that their mother had never so much as considered anyone else; and the whole family had been sustained and kept safe by the great love and devotion of these two. "Marjorie," he called back sternly, "can't you see I'm trying to talk our youngest out of love and back to us?"

"I see it, dear." Mrs. Parrish leaned forward and kissed the top of his gray head. "But you can't do it, Dave," she said, resting her chin on the back of the seat. "Love came to David and Penny, and I suppose it will hit Bobby a wallop, too, when he graduates from the Academy. We were lucky to get Josh MacDonald for our son-in-law and to have Carrol so right for David." She stopped and her eyes grew tender. "Dear Carrol," she said, and added briskly, "Ken Prescott is a nice boy, too. We like him."

"Oh, do you, Mums?" Tippy wriggled around on the seat, glowing and eager to keep the conversation going. "Do you, really?"

"Of course, lamb. Do you suppose we'd make a trip to Washington in this September heat, if we didn't?" Mrs. Parrish laughed. "Or that we would have had him so constantly at the house when we were stationed in Germany, or listened to you sighing over his letters since Dad retired?"

"I didn't sigh." Tippy watched her mother shake out the coat she had used for a pillow, and repeated, "I didn't sigh—did I?"

"Not often." The coat was restored to its hanger by the

window and Mrs. Parrish smoothed it flat, and said, "Most of the time we thought you were interested in Peter Jordon. Are you sure you aren't?"

"Absolutely." Tippy let her chin take its turn on the seat back. "I do love Peter," she said. "When I went up to the Point to dances with him, I tried to tell myself I was in love with him. Last week I almost persuaded myself I might be. Ken was so far away and I wasn't sure he loved me. I *thought* he did, but I wasn't sure. You see," she explained, "I didn't know he had promised Dad he wouldn't let himself get too serious in Germany, because I wasn't quite seventeen then. All last year he hinted in his letters that he liked me a lot, but he didn't *say* too much, he just hinted. And he kept saying he wanted me to go out with Peter—that didn't sound very interested—so I couldn't hope too much; not until he wrote to Dad about coming home, and enclosed a special letter for me. It was all very honorable but, oh, dear," she said, her eyes wide and troubled, "he may not be as serious as we seem to think he is. Oh, Mums, what if he isn't?"

Sudden doubt shook Tippy. It had been a year since young Lieutenant Kenneth Prescott had told her good-by in Munich, Germany. He had said it beside the plane that was to fly the Parrishes home, with the sun bright on his unruly hair, his blue eyes smiling down at her, and only their hands touching. "Good-by, cherub," he had said. "I'm going to miss you." Just that. Tippy remembered his words and forgot the letter he had hurried home to write while she was still flying over the Atlantic.

In her shaken faith, she forgot all the letters he had written and she had treasured since they had parted; and she scarcely heard her mother say, "Stop being silly, darling. Ken wouldn't have asked to come all the way up to the country for a few hours with you, and we certainly wouldn't be taking you to Washington in order to give you a longer time together, if we weren't sure it would make you both happy. You aren't going to *marry* him, Tippy."

"Someday, I am—if he asks me to."

Tippy turned around and slid down in the seat, lost in her own daydreams. Why worry about reaching Washington in a hurry when she could simply sit and be with Ken? That funny double cowlick. She could see it sprouting a stubby fan of hair that wouldn't lie flat, no matter what he put on it. And the drooping slant of his eyes that gave him a sleepy look, so out of character with his boundless energy. And the height of him; and the way he pushed back his army cap and stood regarding her, hands on his lean, flat hips.

The first time he had done that, Tippy remembered, going clear back to the beginning and savoring it, had been on Governors Island, when her father was still in the army and they had lived in the dear white house. Bobby, youthful tormentor and a most unsatisfactory older brother, had been teasing her in front of the Post Exchange. Her outraged screeches had filled the air and had halted Ken like a sudden bugle call. He had stopped to give aid, perhaps save her life, and had ended up staring. Tippy still blushed over the spectacle she and Bobby had made, fighting over the car keys in a battle to the death, then calmly driving off and leaving Ken on the curb. He had been just an officer then, one of several second lieutenants

on the post; but he had always been the one who happened by when Bobby brought disaster upon her. It
hadn't mattered very much until Penny brought him
home and gave him a formal introduction that supplied
him with a name and made him seem very real, indeed.

Penny, the clever actress sister, so happily married to
her producer husband, and mother of two, had remembered Ken as a little boy from long ago on another army
post. She had found him somewhere, brought him over to
her parent's house and invited him to drive back to New
York with her, to see her play. Tippy's rosy glow turned
to grim, unforgiving anger as she relived that moment.

She had been dressed in her green crêpe best, her curls
tied back with a bow; and she had stood in the driveway
with her wooly white coat clutched to her, waiting to
take her place in Penny's car. She was to see the play for
the sixteenth time, with a man. Two seats in the fourth
row center, with a man. Then out flew Bobby and pushed
her aside.

Fifteen regards twenty-two as almost ancient; and except for wanting to hit Bobby right in the middle of his
good looking face, Tippy had felt a surge of relief sweep
over her. It was all mixed in with anger and disappoint-
ment, and it had left her watching the car pull away while
she smiled and waved politely, and wished she had made
a scene.

But Ken had come to her sixteenth birthday dance and
not even Bobby had ruined the sweet torture of that evening. A pleased sigh escaped from between Tippy's lips
and made her father turn his head, and ask, "Sleepy?"
and made her nod and close her eyes again.

That was the last time she saw Ken on Governors Island, for came the unhappy day when she had been forced to leave her own dear country and go sailing off to Germany. Even the discouraging Bobby could stay behind and go to college; and Tippy remembered the tears she had shed and the way her feet had dragged up the gangway, her hopeless surrender in the stuffy, crowded cabin of the army transport. But Ken had been aboard. Happy, busy Ken, off on his first real tour of duty and eager for it.

Tippy slid deeper into her seat and prepared to relive the wonderful year that followed. The wonderful year that had started out to be such a lonely one—and would have been, but for Ken. She had hated war-torn Germany, with its ruined cities and starved, shabby people. She was afraid of wars that could wreck a world, and homesick. There seemed to be no safety anywhere but in America; and she wanted to go home, and be safe. Ken had shown her how wrong she was. He had made her see that war, no matter how bitter and universal, could never wreck the land, the seas, the mountains. He said a little man had told him that. A funny little gnome who had lived in mountains all over the world had sat on his window sill one night and told him that man could never wreck what God had made.

Tippy had believed Ken and his little Man of the Mountains, and had lost her fear. There was suddenly so much to do, so many people to help; and there was dancing with Ken, and skiing, and yodeling their throats hoarse from snow-crested peaks. Either Ken grew younger or she grew up to him, for the days when she saw him were never long enough.

Ken had given her Switzy, too. Little black, French poodle Switzy, bought in the Alps and named for Switzerland, his native land. For a moment motherly concern swept over Tippy, and she said without thinking, "Do you suppose he's all right?"

"Ken? Sure. He ought to be in Gander this evening."

"No, I mean Switzy. I told Trudy to feed him an extra meal today because he was so upset over seeing us pack the car, but she might forget."

"Trudy never forgot in her life." Her father smiled because Tippy's silence had fooled him and her thoughts weren't where he had supposed them to be; and he added, "Trudy has managed to feed all you children since you were babies, so I imagine she can put out a bowl of food for a dog."

"But he's such a little dog."

She sighed again and wished she had brought her curly black friend to see his other owner. Ken had stood beside a sleigh piled high with bear robes and watched her choose one of the five furry balls that nestled there. He had bought Switzy presents, too, a special one on Tippy's seventeenth birthday, and had shipped him home on a transport when her father's old war wound kicked up again and the Parrishes had to fly home to an operation that meant retirement and a serene country life. He always sent a message to Switzy in his letters.

The message usually urged him to be a good dog and take care of Tippy, which was silly, for simply by being the cuddly pet he was, he more than did his duty. He was a constant reminder of Ken.

A large truck loomed up ahead to slow their progress again, and her father chose the opportunity to shift his position and rest his injured hip. Tippy saw him wince with pain as he did it, and said contritely, "Let me drive, Dad. I should have, long ago. Oh, golly, I should have! Pull over beside that tree."

"Now don't get excited." Colonel Parrish felt his wife hanging over the seat again, so slowed the car to a careful stop. "I like to think I'm the man I used to be," he grumbled, as Tippy ran around the car and he slid quickly into her place. "I hate to think I'll be a semi-invalid forever."

"You won't be, Dave." Mrs. Parrish sat back as Tippy released her hand brake and remarked casually, "When you go out to Walter Reed for your check tomorrow, the doctors will tell you how much you can do."

"It had better be plenty."

The car was in motion again and Tippy had no time to resume her daydreams. She and the traffic became enemies, and only her father's sensible caution kept her from blasting the air with her horn. She did try it once, and only annoyed the stubborn driver ahead of her into a pace that was little more than a crawl.

But, at last they crept through the narrow streets of Baltimore and were on the last, long stretch. Signs for Washington's hotels and stores loomed up along the double highway, and she let her foot press down on the gas throttle with pleasurable excitement. She would have only this one more evening to wait, and then. . . . Her father's voice caught her attention and she listened to him say:

"This is one time when we aren't going to stay with any of our friends. We're going to do it up brown."

"How, Dave?" The third passenger was almost in front again as she asked, "Do you mean we should go to the little hotel where I stayed most of the time when you were in the hospital?"

"Nope. I have another one in mind. And we're going to have a suite. Two bedrooms *and* a sitting room."

"Why, David Gerard Parrish! Are you out of your mind?"

"I'm in it," he returned valiantly. "We can't have our daughter entertaining a young man with no place to take him. They can't sit around in hotel lobbies or movies for three days, can they?"

"Oh, it's wonderful!" Tippy let the car leap forward as she gleefully accepted the luxury ahead.

Money in the army had never been exactly plentiful, and now her father's retired pay was alarmingly small. There had been four children to rear and educate and, although Bobby was safely in West Point now, there had been prep school and college for him before it, and she was still on the list for Briarcliff, where Penny had gone. She let herself enjoy a few moments of pleasant contemplation, then said soberly, "We really shouldn't, Dad. Two bedrooms are enough and all we've ever had. I'd worry about it."

"You would?" He looked straight at her, and the laughter lines that recently had been lost in chasms of suffering crinkled out from his eyes. "Then you'd better get over it for I've made up my mind. Haven't you learned, yet, that nothing's ever any fun if you reproach yourself and wish you hadn't given yourself a good time?"

"Yes."

"The wise person," he went on, "figures out what's right to do, does it, and has no regrets. I've been talking it over with myself while you drove. 'Dave,' I said, 'you're due for some fun. You'll get quite a boot out of having a nice living room where your pretty daughter can sashay around, just as if she were in her own home. Perhaps not in the Mayflower or the Statler, but in a very nice hotel you know—with a garden and an orchestra at dinner. That'll give you a bang, too, old boy,' I said, 'so do you think you can afford it?' "

"And what did your other self answer?"

"Well, he took out his mental checkbook, looked it over carefully, and said, 'by gum, we can!' So we are."

"Oh, Dad, you're a darling."

Mrs. Parrish went back into her corner again and laughed happily. "I haven't been so excited in months," she breathed. "Not since Penny and Josh and David and Carrol bought us our house out near them, and gave it to us." She smoothed her brown hair that had gray wings at each temple and sat up straight again. "With Washington so crowded," she asked anxiously, "do you suppose we can get one—a suite, I mean?"

"We already have it."

"Why, Dad, you fraud." Tippy felt very gay and carefree now, for she knew her father had decided everything long before they started, but she did listen to him confess with an embarrassed grin:

"I called up and reserved the rooms, but I didn't do my mental arithmetic until just now. I wanted to be sure I hadn't got carried away and wouldn't have to cancel. We're rolling in wealth."

The car purred. The speedometer ticked off miles like a busy adding machine; and the great dome of the Capitol and the needle of the Washington Monument rose before them as markers for a pleasant path. Tippy swung past the Library of Congress, followed directions her father read from a city map, got lost and went around and around two of the labyrinthal circles which confuse even Washingtonians, and finally pulled up in the private driveway of a dazzling, white hotel.

A boy in a plum-colored uniform rushed out to open the car doors, and she slid from under the wheel on her side and stood on trembling legs. This was the end of her journey. This was where she would see Ken, where her whole future would be decided.

She smoothed her brown Shantung suit, looked at the neat trees along the street, at the hurrying pedestrians, and busy rubber-tired streetcars. The trees boredly dropped their leaves, fluttering them down onto the heads of people who were going stolidly about their earnest business. Motormen fumed at traffic snarls; two little dogs lunged at each other from the ends of their leashes and were jerked back. It was an everyday world, full of everyday people. No one else was meeting a Kenneth Prescott. No one else could be Tippy Parrish, meeting Ken, and so full of happiness she wanted to dance right up the hotel steps and through the lobby.

She was in such a hurry for life to begin that it took

great self-control to close the car door and walk beside her parents to the hotel desk. Once there, it almost wrecked her patience to stand quietly, watching her father sign the registry cards: "Colonel and Mrs. D. G. Parrish. Miss Andrea Parrish."

CHAPTER II

THE THREE Parrishes walked proudly around their hotel sitting room.

"It really is lovely," Mrs. Parrish exclaimed happily, plumping up two yellow damask cushions on a green upholstered sofa, "even though that silly fireplace has make-believe coal that's lighted by electricity and doesn't give out heat. I always wanted an occasional chair like this and furniture with lots of spindly legs."

"You have not." Tippy sat down in the chair under discussion and laughed up at her mother. "You can say you have but you really haven't," she said. "You like our own comfortable, slip-covered and durable pieces and wouldn't trade them for any of the priceless antiques in Carrol's drawing room. The thing I like about *us*," she went on, watching her father put his hat and light fall overcoat in a closet in a small foyer, "is the bang we get out of everything. Good gracious, you'd think we'd never stayed in anything better than third-rate motor courts before. And we've been all over the world and even visited a duke in England—when I was too small to remember it."

"Before you were born," her mother corrected absently. "Before any of you were born, on our honeymoon."

"And we've done the Panama Canal from both directions, and flown the Atlantic, and stayed in the Waldorf —one night and three in a room—and spent a week at

24

the Drake in Chicago—the guests of Gram—but we still
have fun."

"Silly, of course we do." Mrs. Parrish stopped plumping
and rearranging, and considered her quarters. "The place
needs something," she decided. "It looks cold and un-
loved"; and she marched off to the bedroom for her knitting basket.

The basket was a colorful affair she had bought in Italy,
bright with embroidered flowers, and she hung it over
the arm of a chair. Then she set leather photograph fold-
ers on a table. They held pictures of her children and
grandchildren. One showed David balancing Davy on his
shoulders and Carrol clasping a fat Langdon around his
stomach. Another was of Penny and her small daughter in
matching dresses, the two brown heads done in pigtails;
and the last one was Josh, trying to hold his namesake
and the youngest grandchild on a tricycle that would
have been too large for a pygmy. "Now doesn't that look
homelike?" she cried gayly, and turned her head at a
knock on the door.

Colonel Parrish answered it, simply by having a head
start on the others, and came back with two long florist
boxes. "From the kids, I'll bet," he said, ripping off the
strings while Tippy and her mother tore open small white
envelopes that held cards. "I told them we were going
to shoot the works and—yep, I knew it."

Golden chrysanthemums came from Penny and Josh,
long stemmed pink roses from Carrol and David. There
were dozens of them and not enough vases, and Tippy
giggled over the effect they made when the litter of waxed
paper and extra foliage had been cleared away.

"The place looks like a florist shop," she said, standing in the middle and seeing flowers wherever she turned. "Isn't it a shame we can't go up and down the hall selling some, to pay our bill? Gosh, think of all the money we could save."

"That was David's idea. Not selling flowers but giving us this trip; only I wouldn't take it." Colonel Parrish considered what to do with the boxes he still held, then decided to set them in the hall and let a maid dispose of them. "How about going down to dinner?" he asked when he came back. "It's after eight o'clock and I'm hungry."

"I'm not." Tippy sat in her chair again and thought how pretty it was all going to look when Ken came in; and she said, "Dad, you haven't telephoned the Army and Navy Club yet, so Ken will know where to find us when he gets here."

"But I have. They have a room reserved for a General Kresson, others for a colonel and a couple of majors, and one for a very young fellow, named Prescott. For tomorrow."

"Oh, glory hallelujah!" Tippy jumped up and threw her arms around him. "Perhaps I am hungry, after all!" she cried. "I might even let you blow me to a steak."

The dinner was fun. Even pressing her dresses afterward was a pleasant occupation, and she dragged it out as long as she could. She was sure she couldn't sleep; but she must have, for it was bright daylight when her eyes popped open, and her parents were sitting at a small table before their peculiar fire, having breakfast.

"Good morning, darling, and come in," Mrs. Parrish

called, seeing her flushed and tousled in the door. "This is indeed pleasant, and we've ordered enough for you."

"In two minutes."

Tippy's toothbrush scrubbed so fast its bristles made a sea of foam and her comb whacked through her hair and plopped back onto her dresser. "This is the wonderful day!" she cried, dashing back to the sitting room and belting her blue robe tighter. "What time do you think he'll call?" she asked breathlessly, after she had kissed a gray head and a brown one and slipped into her place.

"Not until afternoon, I suppose," Colonel Parrish answered, passing her a plate of toast. "When we flew back, we got into New York around one-thirty, and down here . . . what time did we get here, Marje?"

"About three, I think," Mrs. Parrish answered. "But of course we spent a good half hour at Mitchel Field, talking with the children."

"I can't wait that long." Tippy stretched her arms over her head as if catching stars in her hands. "I'm in such a state. Was Penny as excited when she fell in love with Josh?"

All the Parrish children were accustomed to discussing their feelings with their parents. Happiness always bubbled out of them in gay little fountains; and when they were drenched in a sudden shower of sorrow, they ran for comfort and loving advice. Their father was a yardstick by which they had measured boys, then men; and their mother was always an impartial judge, fair and unbiased. In fact, she was so fair that often a reprimand was harder to bear than physical punishment.

Tippy knew this day meant a great deal to her father. He had told her of the frank way Ken had said to him in Europe, "I'm too fond of her, sir, but you needn't worry about it. I won't let her know it." And the grateful promise he had given in return, at the end of a long conversation: "When the time comes for me to help you, in a couple of years from now," he had said, "you can bet I won't forget it."

This was the way he was fulfilling that promise and showing his gratitude to a boy who had sense enough to know how impressionable and foolish a lonely sixteen-year-old girl could be. Other army girls had rushed into marriage in Europe, other officers had urged them to; and Tippy felt a little resentful because she was being managed by two such honorable men. But her spirits soared when she found her father looking at her over his reading glasses and answering the question she had asked and forgotten.

"In some ways Penny was worse," he said, "because she exploded in all directions. David was the sensible one; and since you're so much like him, it surprises me, child, to have you suddenly become an extrovert."

"I'm completely uninhibited, if that's what you mean," she laughed in retort. "I'm apt to fly at Ken and yell, 'Do you love me? For goodness sake, speak up, because I can't bear it if you don't.'"

"Why, Tippy." Mrs. Parrish laid down her fork with startled apprehension. "Oh, darling," she said with sudden fear, "don't be so tense about it. Don't you think the fine letter Ken wrote Dad, and coming down here and all, might have made you feel just a little bit romantic? You weren't so desperately in love last week."

"Yes, I was. I didn't know it—I was too stupid to know what was wrong with me—but I was. I couldn't make myself love Peter Jordon the way I wanted to. Even when I was up at West Point and sat on a high hill with him, I kept thinking about Ken. Peter's wonderful. He has *every-thing*—but he isn't Ken. I knew I could have a happy life with him, but I couldn't take it. Down in my heart I knew why, Mums."

"But, darling, suppose—suppose Ken. . . ."

"Don't cross bridges, Marjie." Colonel Parrish reached out and patted her hand. "Just trust our youngest and this fine boy who's flying in. They'll work things out. And now, I have to be off to the hospital. I'll take a cab, so don't worry."

Marjorie Parrish sat for a few seconds in silence before she got up and followed him to the door. She saw Tippy happily scooping up marmalade, and whispered, "She's so young, Dave. Penny was almost twenty-one when she married Josh. What if Tippy should insist on getting married?"

"*Tippy?*" He tapped her chin with his finger and smiled at her, his kind blue eyes untroubled. "We don't have stubborn, unreasonable children, Marjie," he said. "Tippy will accept the happiness offered her and wait patiently for more. Ken knows war. He's twenty-four years old, and he knows he has a long tour away from home ahead of him. That boy and I have done a lot of talking, don't forget; so why don't you just concentrate on taking a broken-down old soldier out for a large evening? Give him a bit of night life, huh?"

"Oh, Dave, darling, I almost forgot about you." She laid her head against his civilian coat and wished it could be his uniform with all its array of decorations to scratch her cheek, and cautioned contritely, "Don't let those doctors hurt you."

"I'll tell them you said they couldn't. And I won't be back to lunch."

After he had gone, Mrs. Parrish stood watching Tippy's excellent appetite. Love can do queer things to you, she thought. It can make you eat like a horse or turn pale at the sight of food. Thank heavens, it's affecting Tippy properly for she hasn't any pounds to spare.

Just then Tippy peered into the small, empty marmalade jar and pushed it away. "Do you think it's too hot for my white wool dress?" she asked. The one Ken was so crazy about in Germany?"

"I think you'd melt."

The conversation turned to a woman's favorite topic, clothes, and it wasn't until one o'clock that Tippy sighed and said, "You'd better go on down to lunch. I'm afraid to leave the telephone."

"They have telephones downstairs and you can be paged."

"But I'm not hungry and I don't like this dress. I don't like red with yellow pillows and pink roses, and I look like Merry Christmas when I sit on that sofa. I might have to sit there," she pointed out impishly, "if Ken should want to sit beside me. Just to hold my hand, of course."

She ran over to look at herself in the big mirror above

the mantel. Her startled reflection stared back at her with grave eyes and parted lips. "My soul," she breathed, "what if he should kiss me? What would I do? What would I say?" She whirled around and forgot the careful combing of her short, shining curls as she pushed them back and stammered, "I—I'm kind of scared. I can't remember what Ken looks like. What if he. . . . Oh, dear me."

"Child, you're impossible." Mrs. Parrish considered whether to stoke her own system with food and so fortify it for the afternoon ahead or whether to fade quietly out of Tippy's dilemma. Lunch, followed by a long movie, she decided, would be best for her. She could sit in a theater and not wonder and worry over her husband and daughter, not feel stabs of pain because Tippy had grown up. A movie would be like candy that she could munch, diligent and determined, until it was time to come home.

Tippy missed this last parent after she had left. The fine room seemed so unfeeling. It had held hundreds of lives and crises, a different one every few days, and none had left so much as a scratch on it. She stood in the center of the taupe carpet, in full-skirted and neutral beige by now, and watched an electric clock on the mantel. It was fastened to the wall so no one could steal it, and its hands pointed exactly at two. "Hm," she said, and set the telephone in front of the family photographs on the table.

No ring. Nothing happened. The clock's hands crawled around to three, three-fifteen, three-thirty. How long did it take to drive in from Bolling Field? she wondered. An hour? The careful clock showed long past four. She reached out several times to ask an operator to ring the

Army and Navy Club, but each time drew back her hand and shook her head. Her call and Ken's might cross. She might be holding up the line when he needed it.

She was afraid to sit down and wrinkle her dress, for the little iron on a joggly bed had been hard going, and she was tired of walking about. So she simply stood at the window and looked down on the roof of a garage where mechanics were washing and parking cars.

Washington has trees wherever a tree will grow, and Tippy counted distant trees for a time. She counted the cars on the roof and the number of times the elevator slammed its doors. She listened to a fire siren and strained for a glimpse of the trucks; and finally, she simply stood, twisting the tassel on the window shade and refusing to turn around and learn the time.

"He isn't coming," she mourned. "His plane's been grounded somewhere or the general's making him work. I wish I had the courage to call the club."

Someone in the hall rang for the elevator and she tried to tell herself it was her telephone making that thin, pleading sound. Then the doors clapped open and shut with the silly racket they had been making all afternoon, and she gave a resigned sigh.

Tap, Tap, Tap. The knock was firm and quick, and Tippy turned her head and looked at the door. Mums or Dad, she thought glumly, going slowly across the room. This wasn't exactly the hour she would have chosen for one of them to return, not when something might begin to happen at any moment, but, poor dears, they couldn't wander around outside forever.

She opened the door a little way, then flung it wide. An

officer, cap in hand, stood there. A frond of brown hair waved in the sudden breeze she made, and never had she seen such a look of eager waiting.

"Cherub," he said. And Tippy ran straight into his outstretched arms.

"Oh, cherub, darling," he breathed as his lips met hers; and that was the kiss Tippy had worried about, and a proposal of marriage, all rolled into one.

It was so simple, and so right. No more wondering what one would say. Ken didn't ask, "Are you glad to see me?" and she didn't sigh, "It's been such a long, long time." They merely held each other close in this beautiful moment, then Ken kissed her again and they walked back into the room with their arms around each other.

"That fool plane was late," he said, laying his cap on the table as they passed it, "so Major Lipscomb took my gear on to the club and dropped me off. Oh, Tippy." He turned her around to look at her and asked with a grin, "I wonder what would happen if I let out a yell? The loudest one I have."

"Nothing." Tippy's dimples winked and she said with a shrug, "We might get the fire department or the house detective. We might be thrown out, but it wouldn't matter. Want to try it?"

He flung back his head just as she clapped her hand over his mouth so he kissed her palm instead. "You and I need the wide open spaces," he laughed, "the mountains, where we can yodel to our hearts' content."

"We'll go on a picnic."

"Oh, Tippy, Tippy, darling."

Ken held her away from him and gently cupped her

face with his hands. "You know I love you, don't you?" he asked softly. "It seems as if I've loved you forever; but up to this moment, it didn't matter so much if it was a one-sided love. Now it suddenly does."

"I love you, too, forever and ever. I was going to tell you first if you didn't tell me. I said so to Mums and Dad."

"Is it okay with them?"

"They're glad. Ken," Tippy's arms encircled his neck and it was a natural pose, as she asked, "how long will we have together?"

"Three days. What's left of this one and two more. But when I come back, we'll have all the rest of our lives."

He led her to the sofa where she had been afraid she would look like Merry Christmas. It didn't matter what she looked like now for her feet were tucked under her and she leaned against Ken's shoulder while he explained: "This is the way I figure it. I'll get credit for the overseas time I put in in Germany, so I should be due for rotation in about a year and a half, perhaps a year from this January."

"Not sooner?"

"I don't see how. I've got myself hooked up with a fighting general who seems to have taken a fancy to me and is making plans for my future. Have you cast your eyes on my new bars?"

"I haven't, because I've been so busy looking at your face; but they have sort of dazzled me. Oh, Ken, you're a first lieutenant!" Tippy fingered the bars gently, as if their beautiful silver might tarnish under her touch; and she shook her head when he said:

"I wish I were clear at the top so you could wear mink and diamonds like Mrs. Kresson does."

"It wouldn't be any fun," she told him. "We'd be too old. I like looking forward to all the beautiful things we'll have, and thinking that, someday, I'll be telling people, 'General Prescott says so and so,' and 'General Prescott bought me this.'"

"Darling." He made a better place for her against his shoulder and laid his cheek on her hair. "You're very precious to me," he said. "The most precious thing that will ever be given into my keeping. I want to always cherish you and be worthy of you. Somehow, everything I've ever done since I've known you has been for you. Tippy?" He waited until her head lifted and she could look deep into his eyes before he went on, "There hasn't been any other girl for me in Germany. I went to parties and dances, but that was all. They didn't mean a thing."

"Boys didn't to me, either, Ken," she answered, willing him to understand. "There was Peter—but he wasn't you."

"Poor guy. I needn't have worried about him like I did, need I?"

"No."

Tippy's curls shook but her upturned eyes were still solemn and troubled as she listened to him say lightly, "You know, he scared me green. I liked him, what I saw of him the year he was a plebe and I graduated, and that summer on Governors Island. He was a swell kid. And now he's a football star. I couldn't figure out how stupid old me would have a chance."

"Why not, when you're so wonderful?"

Peter was safely out of the way, explained and accepted; but Tippy spent several more minutes confessing how close she had come to wearing his class ring. "I really tried to," she said honestly. "You were so far away and so much older. I was like you, I suppose. I didn't see how you could want anyone as young and useless as I am."

They covered a whole lost year in the hour they had together; and when a key turned in the lock they held tightly to each other's hand and stood up.

"Welcome, boy," Colonel Parrish said gladly, clamping Ken's shoulder and pumping his hand. "If you hadn't shown up this afternoon, I'd planned to take to my bed with my bum hip for an excuse. This child of mine has driven us crazy."

"Then it's all right with you, sir, for me to love her?"

"It's been all right since you transferred from Munich to Heidelberg because you thought you two were getting too serious." Colonel Parrish's eyes twinkled and he said, "It didn't work, did it?"

"No, thank the Lord," Ken answered fervently. "I've always wanted to tell you how much I appreciated your saying you'd pull for me when the time came."

"Pull?" Colonel Parrish accepted the cigarette that was offered him and sat down in a big chair by the window. "I didn't have to," he said; and Tippy, going over to turn on the lamp beside him, saw how tired he looked.

He was smiling but he looked tired, and she asked quickly, "Oh, Dad, was it bad today?"

"Nope." He blew out a contented puff and relaxed

against the chair's high back. "Nothing's bad," he said, "when you know you have a family to come home to."

He studied the glowing tip of his cigarette and went on quietly, "I want you to remember that, son, and you, too, Tippy. My wife and I love our children. They're deep-rooted in our hearts. But two of them are married now; Bobby's in West Point and will go in the army, and Tippy wants to leave us. We'll miss them—golly, how we miss each one as it goes. There's an empty place that each child leaves, but there's a bigger place that only a wife, or a husband, can fill. When I come home at night, I know Marjorie's there. Nothing in the whole world matters like opening your own door and knowing you'll see the one you love. I want it to be that way with you kids."

"It will be, sir."

Ken's hand found Tippy's again as he went close to the chair; but Colonel Parrish was going on, "I want you each to be sure. Tippy's pretty and you're a handsome lad, but that isn't enough. Too many marriages have been made on looks and dancing well together; and they couldn't stand up under the tough breaks that came along. 'For better or for worse, in sickness and in health,' is a pretty serious thought. Two of our children have already run into it and know what it means. Carrol and David pulled through little Davy's polio, and they did it together. Penny went back to the stage when she didn't want to, because she knew her husband needed her there. They stood the test. Do you think you kids can?"

"Yes, sir, I do," Ken answered. "When the right time comes for us to marry, we have a darn good pattern to follow—the Parrish pattern—and we have a goal of our own."

"We have real love, Dad," Tippy said, sitting on the chair arm. "Pride and admiration are all mixed up in our love. We're *proud* of each other."

"Then you ought to make the grade. Love and pride are hard to beat—but don't lose either one of them."

Another key scratched against the lock, and he sprang up. "Ken's here, Marjie," he called before the door was fully open; then he burst out, "Where, the dickens, have you been? I tried to make sense with the children but, oh, Marje, I've been so worried."

"I went to the movies, dear."

She was quite lost in Ken's embrace. She hugged him exactly as if he were David, or Josh, or Bobby, as if he belonged to her. Then she turned and said, "Oh, Dave, I meant to be home before you came, truly, I did. It was such a long show and I meant to leave any minute, but the feature picture was so sad and I was so happy."

"Logic." Colonel Parrish threw out his hands and looked at Ken. "If you can figure that one out, boy, you'll have a complete understand of women."

"Why it's simple." Tippy linked her arm through her mother's and explained easily, "The people in the story were having a terrible time. They suffered over a lot of troubles, and Mums was glad she has such a lovely life. She simply enjoyed sitting there and feeling happy. Isn't that right, Mums?"

"Of course, darling. It was wonderful to know I didn't have to change places with anyone in that theater, not even the glamorous star on the screen, who, I might say, was very beautiful."

Mrs. Parrish took off her hat, held it out to her husband and smiled when he ruefully studied the bit of felt and feathers. "Funny people—women," he said; and took the hat to the hall closet where it perched on a shelf beside his sensible fedora like a mother bird on a nest.

And so began another glorious hour, with Tippy as happy and satisfied as her mother had been in the theater.

CHAPTER III

"YO-DEL-LA-LAY-HEE-HO-O."

Ken sang the call softly, instead of raising his voice as he had promised himself to do, for he and Tippy were on a very small hill and a very small village was spread out below them. Beyond it, in the smoky fall haze, was a network of highways leading to the Pentagon where his general was receiving a briefing for his campaign in Korea; and beyond that, the broad Potomac and the world's greatest capital.

This was not the perfect spot for a picnic, with a housing development crowding them on one side and a farmer's cows watching them over a fence on the other, but it was the best they could find in their limited time and ignorance of the countryside; and as Ken said, when they finally gave up and accepted it, "At least we can look straight out and not see too much."

They had eaten sandwiches made in a drugstore and drunk milk from paper cups, and now Ken was sprawled contentedly, his back against a tree. He wore a blue sweater of Colonel Parrish's over his army shirt and slacks, and Tippy rejoiced because she had tossed a gray pleated skirt and a bright red blouse into her traveling case at the last minute.

"You know," Ken said lazily, watching her drop the remains of their lunch into her mother's fine knitting basket, "I don't think I'll go to Korea."

40

"Bully for you." She fastened the basket's clasps and crawled over beside him.

"I think I'll just tell General Kresson that I do not choose to go. I'd rather work in the Pentagon."

"Or you might get a job up near us," she suggested, "after they court-martial you. Handy man, or something."

"In striped pajamas, with the stripes going around instead of up and down, and an iron bracelet around my ankle."

They laughed at the silly end of his short bid for freedom, and he made a place for her against the tree trunk, his arm for support and his shoulder for a headrest.

"Tell me about your house," he said when she was comfortable. "I can't go off thinking of you in a Washington hotel when you won't be. What's it like?"

"Well," Tippy considered her home that she longed to show him. "It's just a white house with a garage attached," she decided at last, "with lots of lawn around it and a little brook tootling along in back. It has a white fence with high gateposts and a tin mailbox, where I hopefully look for letters from you. Switzy always comes leaping out from under a rosebush when he hears me at the box, and he always asks, 'Do we have any mail from Ken today?' If we don't, he looks sad and droopy."

"Poor Switzy, I must keep him happy. I'll make it a point to write to him every day. Go on."

"And we have a quaint bay window on the front of the house, with little panes of glass and a wide, wide window seat. Switzy sits there, too, and watches for the postman."

"All alone?"

"No." Tippy's lashes swept up and she looked like a

good little girl caught in the jam closet. "I sit there, too," she confessed.

Ken gave her a hug and let out a whoop that startled the interested cows. "That's a good place for you," he said when things calmed down, "and it might be a fittin' spot for us to stand when we get married. What else have you?"

"Well, we have a long living room. It has a fireplace on the outside wall and two French windows opening onto a terrace. Can you see that?"

"Sort of, if you tell me what color the walls are."

"Green—no, they're going to be gray. We're going to have them painted this fall. And we have rose drapes, long, plain drapes, with cream linings."

She paused to consider the rest of the room and Ken nodded. "Thank you for describing the linings," he said solemnly. "It's most important."

"You're welcome. And there's a big window at the back if you'd care to look out at the brook; and the divan's along the wall, with a love seat. . . ."

"Don't tell me. It's a green velvet love seat and stands straight out on one side of the fireplace. Your father's chair and a round table with a radio are on the other."

"Why, how did you know?" Tippy stared in surprise when he answered:

"That's the way you had it on Governors Island, and don't think I've forgotten. I can get around in that room just fine, but I don't know where to go from there. You'd better take my hand.

She laced his strong brown fingers in hers and held them tightly. "We're in the hall now," she said. "The dining room's over there and the kitchen's just beyond it. The stairway goes up toward the back of the house, then curves around again. At the top. . . ."

"Oh, cherub." Ken dropped all pretense and drew her to him as he groaned, "Will I ever see it? Will I ever watch you run down those stairs, or walk up beside you?"

"Of *course* you will."

"It seems so long. Months and months of cold and snow and rain and fighting. Hundreds of days and nights to live through before I can come back to you. I'll be knowing how everything looks, but not really knowing where you are."

"I'll be right there, darling, waiting. Don't think about it." Tippy knew how much harder it was to be for him than for her. He would be face to face with danger while she sat safely at home, in accustomed comfort. And to divert him again, she said softly, "I have white wallpaper in my room with green leaves on it, and light green drapes —unlined—and the white furniture Penny used to have. And there's a cute little upholstered chair that I'm going to sit in and learn to sew. I'll embroider everything the stores have and put it all in a big chest that's at the foot of my bed. I'll sew up everything from tea towels to tablecloths so I'll be ready for you. And while I'm sewing," she said, "I'll pretend you might walk in or call me up any minute. There's a telephone beside my bed, and I'll sit near it, just pretending."

"I can call you from San Francisco when I get there."

"Will I be home in time?"

"You should be. If we start out at the same time, you should just about make it."

"Then I'll drive every inch of the way because Dad's such a slowpoke. And speaking of Dad," she twisted around to say reluctantly, "I suppose you remember we left him and Mums with the Aldriches at Fort Myer, and promised to pick them up at four o'clock."

"Yes, but we've almost an hour to do it in."

Ken showed her his wrist watch, then turned his palm upward to catch a bright yellow and red leaf as it drifted down. "An orchid for you, Miss Parrish," he said, and gave it to her.

Tippy twirled the stem between her fingers, watching it spin like a bright whirligig. It was a blaze of blended color, and she said thoughtfully, "Once you climbed a mountain to pick me a sprig of edelweiss. Remember?"

"I do. I almost broke my fool neck trying to be a cross between a gay cavalier and a mountain goat. Every time a rock went out from under me I could hear you piping from a good safe place, 'Oh, Ken, be careful.' I've always wondered what you thought I was trying to do."

"Why, I wasn't worried." Tippy looked at him innocently and tickled the end of his nose with the leaf. "I knew you were master of the situation," she said. "I thought you were just doing a sort of rumba to impress me. And anyway," she laughed, "you couldn't have fallen over twenty-five feet. I was right underneath to catch you."

"In a beautiful mess of broken bones. I'll take picking leaves out of the air, it's safer." Ken leaned back against the tree and asked, his voice elaborately casual, "Say, chum, you've got over your crazy notion about war, haven't you? You aren't still afraid it's going to wreck the world?"

"I'm behaving a little better." Tippy tried to sound casual, too, but the subject was a deep one with her, and she drew up her knees and propped her chin on them. "I was pretty unglued when I came back from Europe," she admitted, "and I made up my mind I'd never marry an army officer. I decided I'd have nothing more to do with the army. Your little Man of the Mountain had convinced me that out in the country is the place to be, so I thought I'd take up civilian life and perhaps marry a farmer, like David. Then, somehow, I got all steamed up again, and patriotic, and decided I'd be a WAC and put the world to rights in a jiffy." Tippy ducked her head and peeked at him sidewise as she reached that phase of her mental processes, for Ken had guided her through it via the air mail route; and she felt an embarrassed flush when he threw back his head and laughed.

"Boy, what a WAC you'd have made," he teased.

"That's what Penny told me. She thought it was just as ridiculous as you did, and I don't think I really wanted to be one. I just thought I might enlist and go back to Germany—where you were. I thought, if I could be an officer, we could work together and have fun."

"So I could say, 'Good morning, Captain Parrish. May I shine your silver bars, sir—ma'am? How about a little spit 'n polish today, sir—ma'am?' "

"Oh, Ken."

Tippy's faint flush turned to crimson and he reached out and hugged her even while he laughed. He laughed so uproariously that they both rocked; and, suddenly, she saw it as funny, too. She knew she had planned to be impressive; but it wasn't Ken whom she had wanted to rank, it was her annoying brother, Bobby. And she had to wait until he stopped hugging her with loving little shakes, to tell him so. "Bobby is the most determined, discouraging boy who ever lived," she spluttered. "Look what he almost did to me! By not wanting to stay in West Point and upholding the family tradition, he almost landed *me* in the army. David went through a whole war and only got out because he had to manage Carrol's big estate, so it was up to Bobby to stay where he was. But did he want to? No. He didn't know what he wanted, in, out, or upside down. I decided I'd show him a thing or two and . . . oh, my goodness, wouldn't it have been a tragedy if I'd gone through with it?"

"You wouldn't have. Don't forget that old man Prescott was in there pitching. His hands were a little tied," Ken admitted, "but he pitched a few curves that struck you out."

"Such as?"

"Well, you didn't tie yourself up to Peter Jordon, and you didn't put your signature on any army enlistment blank. What more do you want?"

"You." Tippy leaned back against him and said haughtily, "The whole thing was practically your fault. If you hadn't been so darned honorable with Dad, I wouldn't be in as deep with Peter Jordon as I am. Do you realize," she sat up again to ask, poking her face almost into his, "that I have to go back and *face* that boy, the day after tomorrow? I have to explain to him why I broke a dance date with him, and went off and got myself engaged to someone else. *That's* a fine mess to be in."

"Oh, are we engaged?" Ken hugged her and looked surprised. "Goody!"

"Dope." She pushed away from him and scrambled up. "You're the most unfeeling man," she looked down to scold, "next to Bobby, that I've ever met. Are you worrying because I have to squirm and explain to Peter, and maybe cry a little? You bet you aren't."

"You bet I am." Ken stood up, too, and put both arms around her. "I'm scared witless," he said softly, "of Peter and every cadet in West Point; of every male who even speaks to you on the street."

"You don't have to be." Tippy was contrite, and she stopped her teasing to say soberly, "I'm not going to so much as look at anyone else."

"But you are, cherub. Listen to me." He held her gently, just far enough away so she could see his earnest face, and said. "You're only eighteen. You're in love with a guy who's going to be away for a long, long time. You're not going to sit at home and worry about him; you're not even going to have an engagement ring that will remind others you're tied to him. That's a pretty tough row to hoe. All you'll have is an understanding. Just an understanding that, when he comes back, you'll get formally engaged, with the trimmings."

"I'll get formally married," Tippy protested.

"Huh-huh. You'll get a miniature of my class ring first, and lots of congratulations on snagging off the cream of Korea. Oh, Tippy," he said, into the deep, puzzled amber of her eyes, "don't think it isn't hard not to give you the ring now. Every West Pointer dreams of the time when a girl will wear a copy of the ring that's so dear to his heart. I bought you one, last winter, just hoping, and it's put away for you."

"Couldn't I have it now—please?"

"Nope. You're going to dances. You're going around with Jordon, if he still wants to take you, and your status won't be one bit different from what it was before you came down here. Oh, I know it's rough," he said. "It isn't the way either one of us would want it, but it's the right way. It's the way it has to be."

His mouth was tight as he looked down at her. His eyes searched her face, memorizing each line, each curve and shadow; then he relaxed and said gently, "I'm going into a war, Tippy; but I'm coming back. Your love will bring me back. Just keep thinking and knowing we'll have all the rest of our lives together. We will. And now, since I've lifted this off my chest, let's forget it and go pick up your folks."

Tippy opened her lips to protest the future months he had decided for her, but he had already stepped back and was standing with his hands on his hips. "You're just like Dad," she said rebelliously. "The two of you put your heads together and make an honorable, deciding pair."

"We thank you."

"But I can fool you. I can pretend I'm having fun. I can write you letters that will turn your eyes green, and I won't be doing a single thing I said I was."

"But you won't do it. You'll write me good, honest letters that will make me glad I didn't leave you home to

Mrs. Parrish was running down the porch steps and across the lawn. "Darlings," she called as she came, "we're staying to dinner. The Aldriches want you to come in, but I said they could see you when you come back for us around nine-thirty. Do you mind?"

"It will simply wreck our evening," Tippy answered, leaning across Ken. We do so *hate* to be alone with each other and we never can find anything to talk about. *Couldn't* you keep it a foursome?"

"Silly." Mrs. Parrish pretended to give the car a push, and called back as she turned away, "Have fun—we are."

"Now what do we do?" Ken asked, when they were under way again. "Have you any special place you'd like to go to dinner?"

"I most certainly have."

Tippy knew exactly what she wanted to do, what she had wanted ever since they had looked at houses and played at a make-believe future. It would have to be done in an unsatisfactory fashion, no better than their picnic on a makeshift mountain, but she could do it. "If you'll kindly drive us back to the hotel," she said importantly, "I'll take over from there."

No coaxing could pry out her plans, not all the way back to their luxury suite. And when Ken closed the door, she seemed to forget she had had any, for she said carelessly, "Just sit down and relax, dear," and flopped down on the sofa with a long, comfortable stretch.

"Where? Beside you?"

"No, over there." For a moment her two big eyes regarded him over the sofa back, then she disappeared again and said, "Read your paper for a bit while I think. I have some important thinking to do and I haven't had much time, today."

Ken knew she was playing a game. Just what it might be was not quite clear, yet, but snatches were glimmering through; so he sat comfortably in the chair by the window and picked up a magazine from the table beside him. "Hm," he said, knowing the eyes were watching again. "Have you read this article on the UN?"

"Not yet, I've been so busy."

"There's one on the marriage rate, too. Funny, the things people can think up to write about." Then he laid the magazine across his knee, fumbled about on the table, and casually inquired, "Have you seen my pipe and tobacco anywhere around?"

At that, the whole upper half of Tippy appeared. "You knew what I wanted to pretend, didn't you?" she cried with a joyous catch in her voice. "That this is our house and we're just an ordinary couple coming home?"

"I guess so," he answered, grinning. "But do we have to be so formal about it?"

"Wouldn't we be? Sort of casual, I mean—if we came home together every day?"

"I suppose we might get that way, in time."

"And wouldn't I have to think about what I'm going to cook? Wouldn't you be apt to read while I think?"

Ken considered the enticing picture she made and shook his head. "No, I don't believe I would," he said, preparing to rise. I think I'd rather help you think."

"Stay where you are!" Tippy scrambled off the sofa and

ran to him. "I have to go out for a minute," she said, pushing him back. "And I want you to sit right where you are till I come back. Will you?"

"Sure. But can't I go with you?"

"No." She smoothed down his sprig of hair that only popped up again, so moistened the tip of her finger and pressed it flat. "There," she said. "I'll just get my purse and I won't be gone but a minute."

To Ken, she was gone a long time. A row of shops lined the block beyond the hotel, and it seemed as if she must be transacting business in each one of them. But when she flung open the door, she had only one box.

"Oh, darling, here I am," she cried, and dropped her box as he sprang up to meet her. "I've missed you so terribly. Were you lonesome?"

"I've aged ten years."

A bellboy with a large radio followed in behind her, and she waved a casual hand. "Just put it wherever you always put them," she said. "Lieutenant Prescott and I are staying in this evening and it will be so nice to have it. Ken, dear, have you some change?"

She retrieved her box and was busy somewhere else, so Ken fished a fifty-cent piece from his pocket and held it out.

"Thanks, Lieutenant," the boy said. "If you and Mrs. Prescott want to dance, you can get some swell music from the Statler around nine." And out he went, and closed the door.

"Oh, Ken," Tippy breathed, stopping halfway to the bedroom. "Did you hear what he called me? He said. . . ."

"Come here, Mrs. Prescott, pro tem, and tell me what all this is about. I know we're playing we're married, but why rent a hotel radio, and what's in that box?"

"We're going to have our first dinner at home, and this is the first tablecloth out of my hope chest. I bought it," she said proudly, untying knots with fumbling fingers, "with twenty-five dollars Penny gave me and ten dollars from my allowance. I was going to pretend I was taking it out of a drawer, but . . . see, it has napkins too."

"Cherub, darling." Ken took her in his arms with the long folds of cloth hanging between them. "We'll have a bang-up dinner," he promised tenderly, smoothing back her soft curls and hooking them behind her ears.

She looked like such a little girl, with her face gazing nakedly up to his, untrimmed by its golden circle: so like a little girl trying to play house with a boy who was planning to walk ruthlessly over her dreams. He would spill on her pretty cloth, eat her pretend meal, then say in the careless way of boys, "I think I'll go out and shoot my gun now." Boys always play carelessly with little girls; and men go off to war and leave the women they love.

"Let's see your tablecloth, cherub," he said, carefully putting her curls back where they belonged. And he watched her smooth it out and point pridefully to bunches of embroidered holes.

He saw twice as many holes as there were, for he tried to look at them through a mist that stung his eyeballs. And when his vision cleared, Tippy was saying, "It's cutwork. It came from Italy and I got it reduced. I've ordered our dinner to be sent up, just left in the hall so I can serve it myself, and I have a silly-looking apron in the bottom of the box."

God makes little girls and women, Ken thought, swallowing the lump that stuck in his throat, to be patient and acceptant. Tippy would look at that cloth many times after he had gone. She would touch and love every spot he had left on it; then she would fold it up and put it away again, and wait patiently until he had stopped shooting his silly gun.

"It's a beautiful cloth, darling," he said; and helped her lay it over the little round table.

CHAPTER IV

TIPPY AND KEN were having their coffee before the make-believe fire when the telephone rang. "Oh, my soul," Tippy cried, "it can't be time for Mums and Dad, can it? We've only just finished our dinner, and we haven't *sat*, yet." She looked up at the clock, thrust her cup at Ken, and scrambled across him.

"Hello?" she said; and then, "Oh," and held out the instrument. "It's for you."

The coffee changed hands again; and while she listened to Ken's monosyllabic answers, she rearranged the coffee table before her and admired the two little cups that sat so companionably side by side. She heard a number of "sirs," dropping like periods at the end of each short sentence. "Yes, sir. I understand, sir. Thank you, sir." Then Ken put down the telephone and came back.

"Anything important?" she asked when he sat down again. And she felt quite wifely, returning his cup, hot and refilled, and adding, "I suppose it was one of your bosses."

"Colonel Newton." Ken stirred the black mixture absently, his jaw set and a little muscle twitching along it. Then he turned and said slowly, "It looks as if this will be our last day together, Tippy. The briefing didn't take as long as they thought it would, and General Kresson wants to hop off tomorrow morning."

"Oh, no!" Tippy's little china cup clattered into its

58

saucer. It landed on a slant and knocked off the spoon, but neither noticed it as she cried, "Oh, but he *can't!* He promised you three days. We haven't gone dancing yet, or to the movies with a bag of popcorn, or out to the amusement park. We haven't even just *driven around,* like we planned."

"It's all set, cherub, and there's nothing I can do." Ken took her two hands that were suddenly cold, and said as he rubbed them gently between his, "We hop off at eight; but General Kresson, bless his kind old heart, has wangled an official car for me, and says you can drive out to Bolling Field with me. Just the two of us. We'll go right on pretending."

Tippy sat very still. She sat so long, just staring down at their clasped hands, that he pulled her into the circle of his arms and pleaded, "Don't, cherub. Don't take it like this."

"But I can't help it. I just found out that I'm in love with you. And now . . . oh, Ken!"

"I know, sweetheart, it goes for both of us," he comforted. "The parting has to come, whether it's tomorrow morning or the day after. It wouldn't be any easier whenever we had it."

"But I'd have more—to remember. I'd have one more day to put in my memory book."

"We'll crowd it all in tonight. We can still go out to Glen Echo and ride a merry-go-round, and we might make a midnight show, or . . . wait a minute." He left her and went over to tune in the new radio. "Let's not talk about my leaving," he said when music flooded the room. "Let's dance here, as the bellboy suggested."

He held out his arms, and Tippy went reluctantly into them and stood looking up at him. Ken held her loosely, as if they were on a dance floor and waiting for just the right bar of music, and he said softly, "Little Tippy Parrish; little dearly beloved. I'd rather be cut in pieces than hurt you this way."

"I know you would, Ken. I'm hurting you, too." Tippy sighed and made an effort to explain, "I've never had anything as wonderful as you, in all my life. For two whole years, I've gone around all mixed up and dissatisfied. I didn't know what was wrong with me; and now it's just as if a bright, dazzling light had been turned on and I can *see*." She caught her breath with a little gasp and said as she let it out, "I didn't know love could do this to you. I've never understood why Penny won't stay at our house a minute after it's time for Josh to be home, or why Carrol keeps watching the door for David when I'm telling her something. I do, now. I know how it is to wait for you to come. And you won't be coming again."

"My letters will. I'll be with you every minute in my letters, and they'll be rolling in like clockwork. They'll bring me to you."

Tippy laid her cheek against his army blouse and closed her eyes. Even the blouse which he had dutifully donned before entering the hotel, was a symbol of the army's power over him and her own inefficacy. He had to obey the vast organization behind the uniform and she was but a small bit of humanity caught in its churning mechanism. It was quite hopeless to try to block it, or even hold it back. "I won't be childish again," she promised. "And now, let's dance."

"You aren't being childish, cherub, you're paying me a compliment," Ken said, as they swung across the taupe carpet. "If you'd been tickled pink because I'm pulling out, I'd go off feeling sorry for myself. Instead of that, I feel like a millionaire. I'm more important than General Kresson. I'm the fellow who has the world by the tail."

Sometimes the music was soft and let them drift dreamily around the room or mark time with their cheeks pressed together; and sometimes it sent them spinning into fancy steps and twirls that amused them into applauding their own skill. Neither noticed the clock until the telephone sent Ken racing to switch off the radio and Tippy to answer its summons.

"Hello, lamb, Mrs. Parrish's cheerful voice said. "The Aldriches insist on driving us home, so don't worry about us. If you and Ken will be in, they'd like to come up for a few minutes, but don't feel you have to stay."

"Mums." Tippy kept her own tone level as she explained, "Ken has to leave in the morning. He just had word."

"Dear goodness! Cram in all the fun you can. Don't stay home for the Aldriches, and don't stand there talking to *me*."

The telephone clicked, and Tippy laid it down slowly. How well her mother understood wars. She had told her husband good-by through two of them, and Tippy remembered the calm, busy way in which she did it. But she was *married* to Dad, she thought resentfully. She'd had him for years and years and had led a normal life up to then. None of this "I love you, so good-by" stuff. The first time, perhaps, but not the second. She had four children to comfort her by then.

She stared down at the black instrument, then turned with a smile. "The Aldriches are driving them in," she said. "Our evening belongs to us."

For some vague reason the sound of her mother's voice had strengthened her. Mrs. Parrish had accepted Ken's departure without question and had slangily urged Tippy to enjoy the few hours she could claim. She bucks me up, Tippy thought; like the captain of a football team, when he goes along the line and gives his teammates a slap on the seats of their pants. And she said with a rueful grin, "I'm not the gal my mother is."

"But you're the one for me." Ken caught her and spun her around until glass prisms on the wall brackets chattered among themselves and a discreet knock sounded on the door. Oh-oh," he said. "There's the manager—to throw us out."

But it was only the waiter to take away their dishes.

Tippy helped round up scattered china, the silver warming covers in a stack behind the closet door, the platter on the desk. Ken had carved and served their plates from that platter, and she wished she could buy it and keep it wrapped in the tablecloth. "I don't suppose you would sell . . ." she began, then broke off and watched him carry it away.

"He was most *un*tender with our things," she said plaintively, when the door had closed. "And I didn't like the way he yanked off our cloth and wadded it up any which way, and would have taken it with him if you hadn't grabbed it. But I *did* like the way he said, 'Good night, *madame.*' I did like that."

"Perhaps if we go out someone else may make the same remark," Ken suggested. "Or, if we just ride around, I can throw it in now and then. I'd be happy to call you *madame* instead of cherub, if you like."

"Hm-um! No, thank you." Tippy took the cloth Ken had folded, and laid it carefully in its box. "You make better choices."

"For instance?"

"Let's go for a drive and see if any pop out." She put their two used napkins on top of the cloth and reflected with a swift change of mood, "We've danced together again—I have *that* to remember—so we might ride through Rock Creek Park, singing to the radio, like we used to do; and we might eat hamburgers at some funny little diner, like we've never done; and we might come back here to talk to Mums and Dad a little while, then just sit together as long as we can."

"Right." Ken snapped off the radio. "Would you mind planning the rest of my life?" he asked. "The way you do it exactly suits me."

"It would be a dull life—for a man," she retorted.

The rest of the evening rushed by like a nonstop express that is in a fearful hurry to reach its destination and the time came when they had to say good night. Ken had his luggage to repack, his general to see to; and six o'clock comes early.

After he had left, Tippy sat for a long time before her glowing coals, reliving the precious hours they had spent together; and when her mother paddled in to urge her to bed, she said thoughtfully, "I'm a very lucky girl, Mums."

"I know you are, honey," her mother answered, yawning, "but you'll be a very sleepy one in a few hours. You won't want to get up when the time comes."

"Oh, yes, I will," Tippy sang in answer. "I'd like to sit here all the rest of the night, just thinking of Ken. It's queer," she said, leaning over to turn the switch that controlled her fire, "how much more I know about him than I did two days ago. He's terribly stubborn, Mums."

"Ummm?" Mrs. Parrish blinked and yawned again. She was tired, but she knew Tippy needed a confidante, so did her poor best to look alert and interested. "I've never thought of him as being stubborn," she said.

"But he is. He won't give me a ring and let me be engaged to him. He says I have to go to dances with Peter or anyone who'll take me. As if I give a whoop," Tippy declared, "about dances. Isn't that stubborn?"

"I think it's very wise. He said the same thing to your father and me, and we liked him for it. You're only eighteen," she pointed out, "and you do have a faculty for carrying things to extremes, you know. It would be foolish for you to go out of circulation for a year, or possibly two, and just stay tucked away."

"You sound like I'm a library book." Tippy laughed and left the fireplace. "All right," she said, "you're *all* stubborn—and I give in. Now scoot. You're the tired one, and I'm the gay young thing who is going to dance all night, every night, till dear knows when. Run. I'll turn out the lights."

She felt older than her mother as she watched the pink-robed figure scuttle across the room and disappear. Another electric switch left her in darkness; and she stood for a time, watching the bright pattern a neon sign atop the garage threw on the carpet. "ALL NIGHT PARKING," was what the sign offered; and she wished she and Ken could have accepted it, with the sofa for their garage. Then she yawned and thought it would be good to sleep, knowing Ken was somewhere in the same city.

But she was up at five. Wide awake and up; hanging out her powder blue suit and searching the dull sky for some gleam of light that would predict a fair day. And Ken was there at seven.

His good-by to her parents was hurried. A staff car waited for him outside, and Tippy ran down the hall to punch the elevator bell while he kissed her mother and gripped her father's hand.

"We'll take good care of her, boy," Colonel Parrish said. "You take good care of yourself for us."

"I'll try, sir. Ken still stood, as if there were something more he wanted to say; then the car doors slammed open with their customary gusto, and he repeated, "I'll try," and loped off after Tippy.

"You're a slow soldier," she reproved, standing straight and slender beside him, loving the way he towered above her, and hiding a secret, possessive pleasure in the short sprout of hair that seemed electrically wired to his service cap, popping up every time he bared his head.

"But I'm a demon, once I get under way." The elevator stopped with a sigh and he hustled her through the lobby and out to the pavement, where his driver for the morning stood beside an olive-drab car, door open and ready.

"I usually travel in a jeep," he whispered, when they were seated and their two hands had found each other on the cushion between them. "It's not so stylish but it has more privacy."

"I wish we had one," she whispered back.

The young soldier was too close to them. He sat a few feet in front but was still a member of the threesome, and they felt obliged to carry on a stilted conversation. They discussed their evening before in a cursory way, hoped too long and too fervently for good flying weather, and were launched politely on the air mail service out of Korea when Ken suddenly said, "Oh, heck," and leaned forward.

"Corporal," he asked, "are you married?"

"No, sir."

"Got a girl?"

"Yes, sir."

"Expect to be shipped out any time soon?"

"Any day, sir."

"Then will you please be deaf, dumb, and keep your eyes away from that rear view mirror for about forty-five minutes? I've got a girl, too, and I *am* being shipped out. It's no fun, believe me, not if you're serious."

"I've been thinking that, too, sir, so just forget about me." Two blue eyes looked back at Ken in the mirror on the windshield, then a mouth flashed a toothy, understanding grin. "I have lots of things to think about," it said, "and I don't need to watch the cars comin' along behind me." The mirror did an upward flip and the face disappeared.

"Thanks," Ken said, and leaned back.

His hand found Tippy's again, and he began to talk softly of all the things he had wanted to say.

It was such a short drive; and for once, Tippy applauded every car that held them up and slowed their progress. Long lines of early morning traffic moved bumper to bumper at times, but kept on moving; and the hands of Ken's watch pointed to five minutes of eight when he saluted a guard and they turned into the short road to Bolling Field.

"I suppose I'll go on passing guards for the rest of my life," she murmured. "To enter posts, leave posts, at the commissary, at the movies. Ken," she leaned closer and said, "I'm glad I'm going to stay on in the army."

"I am, too, cherub. I'm counting on you as an 'army brat' to know the social ropes and guide me in the way I should go; to 'further my career' as I heard one wife put it. You know," he changed her clasped hand from his right to his left and put his arm around her, "the army's a family career. We'll have fun with it together, lots of fun. Don't you forget it." A brick building loomed before them, and he said gently, "this is it. This is good-by, Tippy."

"But I thought. . . ." she protested. "I hoped I could go in."

"You can."

He took her in his arms and held her silently. Then the car stopped and he released her, and opened the door. "Thanks, son," he said. "It's been a swell ride."

"I'm glad, sir. I'll park over in the line and bring in your luggage."

"Don't bother. I've only my musette bag and an aviator's pack. We won't need you any longer."

"My mother and father are to pick me up on their way to New York," Tippy leaned over the seat to say. "But thank you, anyway. And good luck to you and to your girl, when you have to go away."

"We'll need it." The young soldier looked at the slim outstretched hand over the seat and the big brown one reaching through the open window. "Gosh, thanks," he said, scrambling out and coming to a smart salute. "I hope I meet up with you again, Lieutenant. If you ever need someone to drive you through the mud in Korea, I'm your boy. Len Donemerski, that's me."

"I won't forget it."

Tippy's heart was beating like a gong as she walked beside Ken through tall glass doors, into a waiting room that teemed with activity. Soldiers, with their duffel bags were three deep around a counter where soft drinks and sandwiches were sold; air force pilots wandered about; officers, waiting for planes or clearance of orders, were in groups; and several women stood near a long glass wall that looked out on the field. Some watched a four-motored plane on the runway, and some anxiously searched the crowded room for someone they loved.

Tippy saw the big plane and her heart did a faster nose dive than it could ever make, but she only said, "Go on, Ken, and do whatever you have to. I'll stay here."

"It won't take long." He turned away, then came rushing back. "I see Mrs. Kresson sitting over there," he said. "I'd like for you to know her, Tip. She's a swell old gal."

"I'd like to." Army training was inbred in Tippy and she

walked unself-consciously with Ken toward a large woman in the mink jacket he had mentioned.

Mrs. Kresson was surrounded by the officers in her husband's group, but she held out a welcoming hand and said heartily, "My goodness, child, I knew your parents before you were born. I haven't seen them in twenty years, how are they?"

"They're fine," Tippy answered, smiling. "Dad was wounded and is retired now."

"What a shame. One of the army's most promising officers. Milton? Come meet this child." Deftly, she passed Tippy around the group.

There were Major General Milton Kresson, bald and florid with keen blue eyes; Colonel Newton, who looked too young for his rank; a major with the weight of the world on his young shoulders; and one who kept casting anxious, undecided glances toward the glass wall.

"I wish I knew how to sneak away from here," he said to Tippy, when the General had turned to Ken. "I'd like a few minutes with my wife, but the old boy keeps me jumping."

"Is she here?" Tippy's eyes followed his nod toward the door; and when he said, "She's the one in the green coat," she exclaimed, "Why, I'll bring her over."

The pretty, dark girl who stood a little apart from the other women started when Tippy appeared beside her. "Did Bert say to come?" she asked, as Tippy explained her errand. "Will it be all right?"

"Of course it will."

"He didn't think I should."

"Oh, come along." Tippy guided her through the

throng which was even greater now and presented her to
Mrs. Kresson with a simple, "Here's another one of us.
This is Mrs. Pierce, and she just told me that she left a
new baby and flew all the way from Arkansas for this
take-off."

The motherly general's wife promptly took Mrs. Pierce
over, so that Ken had a chance to work his way back to
Tippy again.

"Thanks, cherub," he said. "See what I mean about
knowing the ropes? Pierce is a reserve officer and was too
scared to do anything about his wife, but you did. You're
wonderful, darling."

"I'm not." Tippy smiled up at him, and said through
the bonfire of pride he had kindled, "I just know the army,
that's all. I might be scared of the president of a bank, but
not of the army."

There was a stir around them. General Kresson had become the commanding officer again and his wife was rising. All the luggage had disappeared. The crowd near
the door stepped back, and Tippy felt like a condemned
prisoner going to the gallows as she started through the
long lane before her.

"Darling," Ken said, close beside her, "don't forget I
love you. I love you, I love you, I love you. That's for the
next three days, and I'll write another string of them just
as soon as I can."

"I'll keep repeating them. And you know I love you just
as much."

Someone held back the heavy doors and they were on
a long narrow porch. Many people were watching the
General's plane warming up and others behind it, ready

to roll into place as soon as it left, but Ken stopped and turned to Tippy.

"I have to leave you now, cherub," he said, searching her smiling eyes. "You won't cry, darling, will you?"

"Of course I won't." The two little dimples at the corners of her mouth twinkled as she returned his steady gaze. "Army women never cry when they send off their men," she said. "You wouldn't want to remember me crying, would you?"

"Lord, no." He held her close and said into her hair, "It's just that I think I'm crying. Hard. Inside."

Tippy used all her will power to keep the dimples firmly fixed, but she did it. She reached up both arms and clasped them around his neck and whispered, "Good-by, dearest."

It was all over so quickly. His kiss, the tap of his shoes on the steps, his run across the cement to the plane. There was a moment at the foot of it when he turned and waved to her, then he went up more steps and an open door swallowed him.

Tippy kept her smile but it grew set and strained. She kept it for a window in the plane where a hand tapped the glass. The hand wore a heavy, carved ring that looked like Ken's, but the face behind it was too blurred to recognize. The hand kept on waving, and Tippy felt it was Ken's, and waved rhythmically back. She waved all the time General and Mrs. Kresson walked leisurely across the runway, all the time it took them to say a deliberate farewell, while the steps were pulled away and the motors started again.

The big plane was ready to move out on its taxi run;

and for a brief glimpse the doubted face pressed close to the glass. Ken smiled at her, both hands flat against the pane, and she smiled back. Then there was a louder roar of whirling propellers, the plane moved slowly away, and Tippy was left watching a great lumbering giant that was carrying off the dearest one in her world.

CHAPTER V

TIPPY WAS unusually quiet on the trip home. Her mother sat beside her and it was her father's turn to take a nap on the back seat. She was completely silent for the first few miles, concentrating on her driving, and they were almost in Baltimore when she said, "I feel sorry for little Mrs. Pierce, the one I introduced to you."

"Why, Tip?"

"Because she seems sort of lost and forlorn. I don't know why I call her 'little,' " she explained thoughtfully. "She's taller than I am, but she has a kind of picked bird look and her eyes are too big for the rest of her. When her husband was ordered to Germany, she had to stay home and wait for the baby, and then she couldn't start off with it right away. He was sent back before she could get there, just when she had her transportation and was waiting for her port call. She said her trunks were all packed, even the suitcase she brought here; and she's so unhappy because Major Pierce won't get to see his little girl."

"Things don't always work out to suit us in the army," her mother reminded.

"I know it, but it's hard. And the other officers' wives were left in Germany and have to get themselves back as best they can, and only Mrs. Kresson was allowed to fly back with the General. She could have gone all the way to San Francisco if she'd wanted to. I think," Tippy contended, "that Mrs. Pierce should have a chance, too."

73

"Honey, the army isn't run for women, as you should know by now. The plane was for General Kresson, so he could do as he pleased. Just as Dad brought us along when he was flown home. Little people, lieutenants, captains, majors, advance in rank and wait their turn. Can't you see that?"

"Oh, I see it." Tippy returned to her driving and several remarks from her mother brought no more response than a nod of her head.

She avoided all mention of Ken. The trip to Washington might have been made for Colonel Parrish's check at the hospital or a sight-seeing tour. And when they had left the busy Hudson River for a winding side road, and had turned into their own driveway, her father watched her fling open the car door and run to meet a bounding ball of fur that bounced off the front steps.

"Marje," he asked anxiously, "do you suppose she's gone into another one of those withdrawn, hands-off spells about Ken, like she had last year? When she wouldn't even discuss him with us?"

"I don't think so." Mrs. Parrish watched Tippy scoop up Switzy and bury her face in his curly, black wool. "Her love is very new to her," she said, "and she's keeping it locked away inside. I think she's afraid she might cry if she starts letting any of it out—and, I think," she said wisely, "that she's waiting for a spot to cry in. Poor child, she's held back the tears for almost nine hours and the sight of Switzy was too much. Let her alone, Dave."

Tippy stood with her little dog pressed against her and tried to control the sobs that pushed through her lips. Switzy's red tongue licked away the salt drops as they slid down her cheeks, and she held him up for a shield when the door opened and Trudy came out.

"Law, child, it's good to have you home," Trudy said, her brown face crinkled with smiles. But Tippy only held Switzy higher and ran up the steps, past her and into the house.

She was alone in the hall, completely alone. She set Switzy down, let him bounce against her new suit, pawing and yelping his happiness, while she whispered, "Ken, this is the way it looks. Did you see me come into it? Are you thinking, 'now she's home? Now I can call?'" Then she dashed upstairs with the little dog frisking along behind, and flung herself on her bed, face down.

"Oh, I miss him so, I miss him so," she wept into her green counterpane, while Switzy brought his ball and sat up with engaging patience, waiting for the romp they always had when she came back to him.

It seemed a long, long time before the telephone brought her head up with a jerk, hours and hours and hours, instead of only one. Her face was streaked with tears when she reached for it but laughter bubbled out when an operator said, "San Francisco is calling *Madame* Parrish," and Ken cut in with, "Hello there, cherub."

Fifteen minutes flew. Fifteen minutes went by on wings with Ken constantly saying, "Oh, hang expenses. Operator, *please* keep off the line." His A.P.O. number was given and memorized for lack of a pencil; Tippy repeated her rural delivery route, and even Switzy talked. His conversation consisted of a surprised yelp when Tippy pinched him.

"Did you hear him?" she cried excitedly, pleased to

have brought forth some response to Ken's whistle and glad he couldn't see the indignant dog disappearing under the bed.

"He didn't sound too happy to me," Ken answered. "Uh-oh. Here comes the major. You know, the busy, worried one. Wait a minute."

She could hear a door rattle open, then his voice came back. "He's just looking for a place to call his mother, but I think he's found one."

"Are you in a phone booth?"

"I'm in a beaut. I wish you could see it. Soldiers have scribbled names and addresses over every inch of the walls and the seat's so busted I feel as if I'm perched on a hunting stick at the races. Say, have you ever been to the races?"

"Hm-um, I never have."

"We'll go when I come back. Remind me to ask you for a date, preferably on the first night I'm home, so we can. . . ." His voice trailed off again, then said with startling clarity, "We're off, Tip. Pierce just came after me. I'll cable from Honolulu if I get a chance, but don't count on it. Pierce says the General wants to go aboard so that means little Kenny has to hop to it."

"Ken? Oh, darling, I love you."

"I love you, too, with all my heart and life. Good-by, cherub."

The connection was cut and Tippy was left holding something dead and black.

Her tears were over. She had heard Ken's voice again. The room was filled with it; and she lay on her back, arms crossed under her head, listening to the words that were all around her. He had been in this house, in this room, and she felt it could never be such a lonely place again.

"I talked to him!" she cried, when she ran downstairs and found her mother in the living room with a tray of supper. "Mums, it was *wonderful!*" Then she saw Trudy standing beside the piano, and flew at her. "Why, how do you do," she greeted, rumpling Trudy's starched white apron as she hugged her. "Did you know you're going to teach me to sew, and to darn and mend? Well, you are."

"Law, child," Trudy answered calmly, putting herself to rights again, "you can't stick a pin in straight, let alone a needle. I'd take to my bed if you was to mend something."

"Then make ready for a long relapse. *I* am about to start on an endless sewing bee."

The French toast and syrup her mother was having smelled good, and she went over to sniff it. "I'm hungry," she said. "I'm hungry and I'm happy, because . . ." she threw her hands above her head and sang from one of the popular tunes on her record player . . . 'I'm in love with a wonderful guy.'"

"You sure are unrestrained about it," Trudy said dryly; and Tippy missed the satisfied nods she and Mrs. Parrish exchanged, for she went on, "I reckon, if you're goin' to carry on such gymnastics, you'd best come out to the kitchen and eat something to keep up your strength."

"I'm right on your heels, my love."

Tippy sat at the kitchen table and poured syrup over her fried bread with a lavish hand. And when Trudy had gone off and left her, she fed bites to the faithful Switzy. He was full of his own good horse meat and only took them to be polite, and because she kept up such a running fire of delightful chatter.

"We have a lovely, long evening ahead of us," she told him happily, "and I think I should start telling people about my good fortune."

First, not counting her immediate family who knew why she had gone to Washington, there was her best friend, Alice Jordon. "*Jordon!*" Tippy gasped. Alice was Peter's sister! And she looked down to inform Switzy, "It's an unfortunate relationship. I don't think she's going to be much thrilled, do you?"

Switzy yawned his reply which seemed a satisfactory answer, for she nodded and agreed, "You may be right. She's so in love with Jonathan Drayton that she may not mind. And she didn't fall for Bobby when he was so crazy about *her*. She just fluffed him right off, even though we'd sort of promised to be sister-in-laws, someday. She let me down first, didn't she?"

Switzy had found what he hoped was a flea and was nipping at his wool with such pure joy of torture that Tippy gave him a push with her toe. "Stop that," she ordered. "Nice dogs don't have fleas." And she returned to her musing. Alcie would understand, she decided. And even if she didn't, she would have to accept it. Now was the time to tell her.

The new electric dishwasher hid her plate and glass in its hygienic cavern until morning, and left her free to run up the stairs again. She hated to let any other voice come into the room where Ken's had been, so stood with her hand on the telephone, reluctant to use it. "Silly," she said and shrugged. "No one can possibly crowd him out."

And she listened for the local operator to dial New York, then the small army post of Governors Island.

It would be more fun to tell Alcie in person, she reflected, while she waited for someone in a whole houseful of Jordons to answer a telephone, and see the surprise on Alcie's face. She would push back her straight, brown bang until it stood out like a thatched roof, and her big gray eyes would grow larger and larger. Tippy almost hung up. Then a familiar voice spoke and she cried, "Hi! I'm home again."

"Home? From where?"

"Dear me." More explanation was needed than she had expected to give. If Alice didn't know about the trip to Washington it meant that she hadn't talked with her brother. Peter knew. He hadn't told; so she would be waiting for the news with a completely open mind. Tippy prepared to state her cause with a few carefully chosen sentences, and began by asking, "Didn't I tell you I was going to Washington?"

"You couldn't. I was away myself last week, remember?"

"Oh, sure. Well, it's been an exciting trip." Tippy let an impressive pause take up some time, then asked, "Alcie, are you still so much in love with Jonathan?"

"Silly," came back, "of course I am. How could I change in a week?"

"I mean—does the whole world look different now? Are you excited, then calm, then jumpy, and almost . . . almost bursting with joy?"

"Listen." Tippy could almost see Alice's puzzled frown in the telephone; for she asked, "What's wrong with you?

Are you still worrying about Bobby? If you are, don't. He got over carrying the torch for me ages ago."

"It's not Bobby. It's—me."

"Then why don't you come in and stay a couple of days?"

"I can't. I just got home. Why don't you come out here?"

Alice's laugh rang out. "Tippy," she said, "you sound like a nut."

"But could you come?"

"Wait a minute and I'll see."

There was nothing but silence on the other end of the line and such a long wait that Tippy could count too many nickel's worth of time being chalked against her; but at last Alice came back from consulting her father, checking on four small children and two maids, and announced, "Dad doesn't need the car so I'll come."

"*Tonight?*"

"Isn't that when you wanted me? It's only a little after seven and I can be there by half past eight. The turnpike's lighted most of the way."

Tippy always forgot that Alice was so competent. She looked so childish, with her straight brown hair and bang. Somewhere in the middle of nine children, in three assorted sets, she had to be competent. The eldest daughter had married and taken two of the children to live in England; the second had eloped and was busy upsetting her husband and Hollywood; Peter was in West Point; and that left Alice at home with her father and a complicated household. "Now don't start 'jumping' or get becalmed," she said. "I'm on my way."

Alice could be told in person! Tippy slammed down the receiver and went twirling about the room. "Ken's somewhere out over the ocean," she told Switzy, who had gone to sleep in his basket, "and I'll be making my first announcement of my *almost* engagement. Oh, joy!"

She had an hour and a half to spend on a letter to Ken. Her pen went racing over the thin airplane paper she had used for his letters in Germany, and she looked up with a blank stare when Trudy came upstairs and stopped in her door.

"Honey," Trudy said, "that Jordon boy's been callin' up every night at about this time. He either don't get it through his head about you an' why you went to Washin'ton, or else he don't give up. I reckon he's apt to call tonight."

"Oh, but he *can't!*" Tippy pushed her paper back on her white desk with a groan and slid around on her chair. "I don't want to talk to him."

"I reckon you has to."

"But what can I say? I told him why I broke my week end date. I told him Ken was coming home. From the way I breathed Ken's name he ought to know."

"But he don't. He jus' keeps on callin' up, as polite as can be, an' always askin' when I expects you back."

"That's a pretty kettle of fish."

Tippy sighed and looked at Peter's picture on her dressing table. His clear gray eyes looked back at her from a rather long face, his mouth and jawline firm above a stiff cadet collar, his light hair neatly parted and lying flat as hair should do. It was not a handsome face by any standard, but it was dependable and directly honest. It was completely Peter.

"What you goin' to tell him?"

"I don't know." A lot of girls would be glad to have him back in circulation again. Tippy had watched innumerable girls hang around and bat their eyes at him after a football game, and she said with a sigh, "I'll give him back to the gals, I guess."

"Is that what's goin' to happen to him?"

"What else could?" She was a little annoyed with Trudy for being so dense. "I'm engaged," she said primly. "Don't you know what that means?"

"I naturally does. I was that way once, myself, an' I got married. Of course I didn't have no other beau to worry about," Trudy conceded, watching Tippy carry the facsimile of Peter over to the bookshelves and set it beside one of Bobby in disreputable slacks. "It's hard to know what to do, child," she said, looking at the lone photograph left on Tippy's dressing table. "From what your mama tells me, Mr. Ken is a fine boy, but so is Mr. Peter. It don't seem fair, with the world so full of bum ones, that they should both want the same girl, does it?"

"No." Tippy went back to her desk again and sat considering her blue shoes. "I wish I knew what I'm going to say to him," she worried.

"Mr. Peter'll help you in his nice quiet way. Good night, child," Trudy answered, and went rustling down the hall.

Tippy thought of that last remark when her busy telephone rang again. She hoped it could be someone asking for one of her parents; but when Peter's deep voice said,

"Hello, Tippy," she only hoped Trudy had been right and he would make the conversation easier for her.

"How was Washington?" he asked. "And how was Ken?"

"*Won*-derful!" She said the word like a prayer; and told herself, "Now *that* should tell him."

But it didn't, for he went on, "I'd like to have seen him. I've been calling up every night, thinking he might come home with you, but Trudy didn't seem to know what your plans were."

"He's gone to Korea."

"Yeah, I gathered that. One of the officers up here told me that General Kresson never wastes much time. Ken's sure a lucky guy to have that old boy pick him."

Such a thought had never occurred to Tippy. She had been concerned with the result of Ken's assignment, never with its cause; and she stammered, "You mean—you mean—because he's good?"

"You have to be good if Kresson wants you. I hope I can get a break like that someday."

There was Peter, praising Ken as she had never done. He saw this new assignment from a future officer's point of view and envied it. Tippy forgot to listen to the rest of what he was saying, while she sat in conscious-stricken misery. She hadn't praised him enough. He was always telling her how wonderful she was and how proud she made him, but had she told him? She wanted to call back the plane or shout across the Pacific Ocean, "I'm proud of you, darling. I'm proud of the job—I'm proud of *you!*" But she could only sit gripping the telephone with both hands while Peter asked, "Are you still there?"

"Oh, Peter." The telephone went up where it belonged and she groaned into it, "I didn't tell Ken how wonderful I thought the job was. I didn't say it, Peter, not once. Not the way you are. I just thought about myself."

"He knew you thought it, Tip. I wouldn't worry about it, he knows."

Everything was backwards. Peter was being the comforter and she the comforted. He was even consoling her by saying, "Don't feel bad about it, Tip. You didn't have time to say everything you wanted to, so you can put it in a letter. Can you hear me?"

"Yes—I hear you."

"Then buck up. I wish I could see you this week end but that's another thing I've been wanting to tell you. The team leaves Friday for our first game away from home and I'll have to study like the dickens before I go. Next week end, huh?"

Tippy stared at the telephone unable to believe her ears. Peter sounded exactly as he always had. Perhaps he hadn't understood her frenzied sentences. Perhaps he didn't know how final her loving Ken made things. And she began all over again, "Peter, I think I ought to tell you. . . ."

"Don't try. I get it, Tip. Want to come up next week end?"

"Why, I'd like to."

"Same place, same hour. I'll see you then."

She sat holding a telephone gone completely crazy. "That was Peter," she told herself. "Believe it or not, that was Peter who once begged me to marry him. And now he sounds as matter of fact as a dictionary. He sounds like a brother or just any old friend. Well, blow me down." And she went back to her letter to Ken.

She had so much to tell him now, due to Peter; and her pen went racing back and forth across the paper like a recorder out of control. Pages littered the blotter when her mother called from her room, "A car just came in the driveway. It looks like the Jordons'."

"It is."

Tippy ran down the steps, skipping some and just barely touching others, and made the front door just as Alice reached for the knob. "Come in here!" she cried. "Let me take your case and your coat."

Alice dutifully set her overnight bag on a chair and was about to hand over her green topcoat when Tippy grabbed her. "I'm in love!" she cried. "With Ken! I've been to Washington to see him and I'm utterly *delirious* with joy!"

Alice did exactly what Tippy had expected she would. She pulled loose and pushed her green hat back on her head. Her bangs went with it, and she stared like a horror cartoon. She looked so startled and so funny that Tippy hypnotized her further by saying, "I'm going to marry him—the minute he comes home from Korea. Now what do you think of that?"

"Gosh." Alice came out of her trance with a bang. "*Are you serious?*" she cried.

"I am."

"You're not just having another one of your romantic notions?"

Her gray eyes looked as big as they could get, but Tippy knew she could open them even wider. And she did it by saying, "Ask Mums and Dad if you don't believe me. Ask Peter."

"I can't grasp it. I'm knocked all in a heap."

She sat down on the chair, right on top of her small case, but Tippy jerked her up again. "Come in the living room," she ordered joyously, "and I'll tell you so much that your own romance will look pitifully dull."

She led her addled guest across the hall and loved her dearly. Alice was a much more satisfactory audience than Peter.

CHAPTER VI

"This is a queer kind of a life," Tippy remarked, coming into the living room after she had been home from Washington a week. "Oh, I'm not complaining," she added hastily, seeing her mother's surprised look. "It's just that the tempo of things has slowed down, that's all. I can't expect to live in rousing excitement all the time. But school? A prim girls' school? Ugh."

"School seems dull because you played all last year, honey," her mother said, laying aside her book. "It's hard to study again and fall into a routine. Briarcliff is a nice school."

"Oh, it's nice, all right." Tippy sent out a hollow laugh and plopped down on an ottoman, where she hugged her knees and complained, "There's nothing nicer than a junior college that has high school kids loping all over the place and teachers constantly telling me how darling Penny was. Really, if I hear any more about Penny I'm going to quit."

"What did you hear about me?"

Penny's voice called from the hall, and she came strolling in to scold equably, "This is a fine welcome for a busy woman who's left her home and children to give her family an hour of her precious time."

"We didn't see you drive in." Tippy swung around on her stool and thought it no wonder the teachers wished they could turn in the dull blonde for this sparkling brunette. Penny's brown eyes were soft and laughing. Her bronze hair swung free, long enough to be caught up in the cluster of curls she wore in her play, and she was thoroughly enjoying a piece of Trudy's homemade bread with strawberry jam smeared across it. "Believe me, babe," she said, "you don't know how good you have it. Any news from our hero yet?"

"One letter. One measly little letter, posted in Honolulu." The conversation had switched to a better track and was headed somewhere pleasant, and Tippy invited, "Take a look at my sewing—it's on the piano."

"Sewing? You? Great jumping ghosts!" Penny licked her fingers and winked at her mother. "This I must see," she said, walking over to inspect a square of white linen that had purple and red blotches scattered over it. "What are those?" she asked, pointing.

"They're going to be people, when I put more colors in. I do all one color first. It's a Mexican pattern."

"You slay me." Penny turned back to Mrs. Parrish without giving the cloth a just inspection, and remarked with a shrug, "No wonder she doesn't like college. She should be in a domestic science school. How did we ever get such a funny child?"

"Love dood it," Tippy answered for her mother. "Love turned me into a nice little homebody. I sew a while and knit a while, and then I. . . ."

"We'll have to start calling you Beth, for Beth in *Little Women*," Penny interrupted rudely. "Well, Marmee?" She clasped her hands behind her back and strode over to the fireplace. "Christopher Columbus," she quoted, toasting her rear before an empty grate and looking so like Jo that Tippy wished she could see her play the part on the stage or in a movie. And she caroled, "I must be off to find my Laurie."

"Can't you stay to lunch?" Tippy begged, hating to lose this unexpected sunshine.

"I can't." Penny was Penny again and she shook her head. "I left Josh in charge of our young and we have to be in town early. Tomorrow's a matinee day so I won't be out tonight. Josh said he'd try to come but he has an appointment in the morning that he may have to keep. Acting is a queasy, woeful business," she said dolefully.

"We'll keep an eye on the children," her mother answered; and Tippy offered quickly:

"I'll go over and stay with them. I can study there as well as here. I can study there as well as anywhere," she said, looking grim. Then she laughed and added, "I can sew while I sit."

"I'll take a rain check. Minna and Lucy are reliable servants, but I do thank you, cherub."

"Cherub" had been Penny's nickname for Tippy long before Ken had appropriated it. It seemed strange to hear it now, on any lips but his, for once stolen, it belonged only to him; and it made Tippy sigh and say, "You're darned lucky, do you know it?"

"Of course I do. And now, farewell. 'Parting is such sweet sorrow.'"

"Please," Mrs. Parrish protested. "I can't go from Louisa M. Alcott to Shakespeare in such a few minutes. Let's just be us for a bit."

"Us?" Penny turned and asked with surprise, "Who wants to be anyone else?"

"I do." Tippy smiled up from her ottoman. "I want to be Mrs. Kenneth Prescott," she pointed out. "The rest of you may be very well satisfied with your lives and husbands, but I'm sitting around, just waiting."

"Have patience, lamb." Penny bent over and kissed her. "We've all been through it, so have patience."

Tippy tried to have it. She went dutifully off to school each morning in a small coupé David had loaned her and tried to make her studies seem as important as her plans for the future. *"I suppose,* she wrote to Ken, *"it's as necessary to learn Latin as cooking. Since you're so well educated, of course I must be—but I must admit, I was a lot prouder of the apple pie I baked with Trudy than the paragraph of Cicero I translated. The pie turned out to be a dream but the translation was a nightmare. Oh, brother, am I bored!"*

It wasn't until the following week end that she understood Ken's determination for her to go to dances and be a part of the world she had known. In spite of herself, she felt a thrill of excitement as she packed her case for the trip to West Point.

"It doesn't mean that I'm keen on seeing Peter again," she explained to Trudy who was handing her things, a freshly laundered blouse, her blue dance frock, and gold sandals. "It's just that I get so tired of being stuck out here in the country and commuting to Briarcliff and back. I'll even be glad to see Bobby—if I happen to run in to him, which I probably won't. If he has a girl up for his dance he'll do his level best to avoid me. But football games are fun, being with the star of the team and milling around in the crowd and feeling young. I love Ken just as much, but I'm glad I'm going somewhere. That's natural, isn't it?" she asked doubtfully.

"It's the way it should be," Trudy answered, folding a slip and laying it in the case. "Take me, for instance. I loves it here with your mama and papa and you, but I'm mighty glad when prayer meetin' night comes around an' I can go off with my friends. I goes to church an' you goes to dances, an' we both has lots to talk about when we comes home."

"And I'll have more to write to Ken about. I suppose he might get tired of reading about cross-stitching and a cake mixture you can buy in a package," Tippy said thoughtfully. "His letters have been full of interesting things he's seen and conversations with interesting people. I did write about funny Miss Abernathy who teaches physical ed.," she said, closing the lid of her case. "She's the only teacher in the whole school who makes good reading, and I even had to pad her up a little. Men like football. Ken will be more interested in West Point and the officers I see there than in a girls' school."

She stood looking down at her neatly packed dresses with such a troubled face that Trudy said quickly, "Child, you don't have to persuade yourself into goin' to a dance. Mr. Ken wants you to go, he said so. Don't get squeamish, now that you's made up your mind. Go an' enjoy it."

"All right." Tippy allowed herself one more reluctant sigh before she picked up the short ermine jacket Penny had given her for evening wear. "I'm off," she said grimly. "I'll enjoy it or bust."

She was a little uncertain all the way to West Point. Her small car purred along and seemed happy not to be

taking the familiar route to Briarcliff. It put a holiday
bounce in its tires that gradually began to cheer her;
and by the time she had reached the guard at the Academy gates, her heart had started pumping with the same
crescendo. They slowed down together, the motor to a
leisurely pace, her heart to a jouncy nervousness over
meeting Peter.

Everything was changed since her last visit. Peter had
been almost sure of her then, she had been almost sure of
herself. She had driven home thinking of him and wondering if really he weren't the right one for her, wishing
she had told him so, vowing she would give in and tell
him soon. Then a beautiful star had exploded over her
house. Ken was coming home. Ken loved her.

Tippy squirmed on the seat. Grant Hall, meeting place
for cadets and their girls, loomed ahead of her. She must
either swing in to the curb or drive on past. One more
turn around the drill field, she thought, might calm her.
It would give her time to think up a greeting, not too casual, not too stilted. She saw a familiar gray figure in a
crowd of gray figures and bright coats on the steps and
knew she was caught and would have to swing in. "Oh,
dear Gussie," she groaned in panic. "Do I say, 'Hello,
Peter,' in a kind of serious way, or do I just say, 'Hi,' like
a nut? Oh, gosh!"

Peter had watched her wavering progress along the
street, and he detached himself from the group he was
in and came out to the curb. "Hello, Tip," he said, opening the car door and grinning at the wax figure inside. "I
thought you never would come."

"Oh, hello."

Tippy gulped and came to life as he asked, "Want to come into the Boodlers for a soda or go on back to the hotel and leave your gear?"

She looked at him and thought, He's so darling. If I'd been Alcie, I never could have been as nice to me as she was. I'd have hated her for the rest of my life. "I think," she said, "maybe—I'd like a drink."

"Okay."

He waited while she found her purse and the gloves she never wore but always brought and dropped until he kept them inside his cap that was his only pocket, then took her hand in the accustomed way and led her across the walk to the steps. "We're counting on you for touchdowns, Pete," a cadet said, while two others slapped him on the back and a pretty girl asked in a soft pouting drawl, "You ahen't fo'gettin' the dance yo' asked me fo', sugah, ahe yo'?"

"You bet I'm not," he answered. "It's the sixth," and piloted Tippy through the mob.

Everyone was a stranger. Several spoke to her; and the pretty girl said, "Hi, Tippy, honey, I reckon you don't mind mah makin' suah of Petah, do yo'?" but they were strangers, nevertheless. Peter's hand scorched around hers like a hot iron, and when they were inside the door, she pulled him to a stop and said, "Peter, it's selfish for me to come up here."

"Why?" He took off his cap and held it out for her gloves, and asked with his gray gaze level, "Because you think you should tell me what the score is?"

"Not exactly that." Noisy voices shouted in the soda fountain just beyond them, and she began walking past its open door, along the corridor to a large reception room at the end. It was quiet there, deserted on this mad morning before a football game, and she sat down on the arm of a sofa and said in troubled thoughtfulness, "If I stop coming up here you'll drag other girls. So many girls want you, Peter. You're the most popular man in the corps, or you could be if you'd let yourself, and if I'd stay away."

"But I don't want you to. You may be in love with Ken —and I've always had a feeling you were—but I'm in love with you. I want you here. I want to see you as much as I can. That's all there is to it, Tip. I simply want to be with you."

"But it isn't fair," she protested.

"Fair or not, it's the way I like it." He stood before her, tall, straight and slim, in his gray uniform. "Do I look like a miserable guy?" he asked.

"No," she had to admit.

"My color's good, I eat well, my football hasn't slacked off enough for the coach to fire me. If I feel okay I don't think you should try to be a doctor, do you?"

"No."

"Then let's forget it. I think Ken Prescott's swell. If you love him, he must be even better than I think he is and I wouldn't try to crash his time. I want the best for you, Tippy," he said earnestly. "I've told you that. I'll admit I'm sunk over not having you myself, but if it has to be this way, I'd rather lose you to Ken than anyone I know."

"You—you won't keep hoping." Tippy made a statement instead of a question because she wanted him to agree with her, but he only grinned.

"You bet I will," he said. "Oh, I won't mope and make you feel sorry for me, or put you on the spot," he amended into her troubled upturned gaze, "but don't cut me off completely, Tip, that wouldn't be kind."

"All right."

Tippy knew they had got exactly nowhere. Peter looked cheerful enough but he had said puzzling things. He still loved her. He wanted her to have Ken if she wanted him, yet he did want her himself. She let her breath out in a weary sigh that made him pull her up.

"Stop worrying," he scolded. "Really, you do more worrying than any ten people I know. Now you've lost that drink I promised you and you'll have to have an early lunch because I'm due back with the team. See how worry fixed you up, and trying to make big gestures?"

"I had to be honest," she protested. "I had to tell you—it's Ken."

"So you've told me."

Peter walked her back along the corridor, back to her car; and it wasn't until he slid onto the seat beside her that he said, "This is a swell day for a football game. I bet it'll be hotter than the hinges for the teams, though. Which reminds me: I had your chrysanthemum sent up to the dragon who guards your floor. She has about a hundred of them, so check with her. She has your flowers for tonight, too."

Alone in her room after a hurried lunch, Tippy looked at the two florist boxes on her bed. One held the usual golden ball with its gold and gray and black ribbons, and the other, pale pink camellias. "An orchid for you," Ken had said, catching her a bright, floating leaf. And in the midst of all her pleasure, a tear dripped down on the green waxed paper and she walked over to the window.

Girls screamed their good-by's below her as cadets clapped on their caps and took off on the run, to make parade formation and march onto the field with the corps; horns blared, and the older crowd milled around. The whole scene was happy bedlam. No one cared about the Korean War today; and Tippy looked down to tell them softly, "We won't either—next year, when Ken comes back."

CHAPTER VII

IT WAS an odd week end. The sparkle of being at the great Military Academy was gone for Tippy, but she was interested and busy. "And I did see Bobby," she told her parents, in the midst of relating events to them.

"How does he look and what did he have to say?" her father asked.

"He's just the same."

Tippy tucked her feet under her and considered the lanky brother who had pushed through the crowd outside the stadium after the game. She had been with two other girls who were waiting for players to dress and meet them when she heard the familiar shout of, "Hey, stupe, hold it." And there was Bobby, waving his cap at her.

Tippy thought him a poor copy of David. His bright, curly hair matched David's but it was clipped too short. His eyes were an electric blue instead of a proper azure, and they had an uncomfortable way of outstaring a person. Even when he was wrong, and especially then, Bobby could stare innocently and interminably. He could make Tippy squirm and want to look away when she knew she was right. Now she turned back from the girls and told him irritably, "Stop shooing at me as if you're rounding up the herd. I brought your cake. It's in the back of the car."

"Did you bring the rest of the boodle I phoned for?"

"Just the cake. That's all Trudy gave me."

"Well, gosh darn it." He clapped his cap back on with an offended glare. Then he leaned against the stadium wall and asked, "How've you been?"

"Just fine."

He looked innocent and sweet leaning against the wall, one black shoe crossed over the other, his stiff gray blouse wrinkled out from his flat chest, and Tippy did one of her usual emotional reverses. "I heard Mums telling you about—Ken," she said, and might better have presented him with a double-barreled shotgun.

No felicitations on her recent engagement came her way. She got the blue stare. And he banged away with, "Whatever made you give Peter the brush-off? My gosh, you dope, he's worth a hundred of any other guys!"

"I happen to love Ken, Bobby."

"I don't believe it."

Peter was his hero. Unlike the rest of the corps that passed fourth classmen as if they were invisible, or, with sudden, sadistic delight, dreamed up endless ways to torture them, Peter had spoken to Bobby last year. He had pulled him through a bad time of not knowing what he had wanted to be or where he wanted to go, and had turned him into a good cadet with a corporal's stripe on his sleeve. Tippy could understand why he yelled now, "You're turning down the grandest guy that ever lived!"

"I think so, too, Bobby," she answered soberly. "I've had to decide between two grand guys. A girl can't help loving one more than the other."

"*Girls!*" He threw out his arm in one of his sweeping gestures that sent petals flying off her chrysanthemum, and growled, "First Alcie, then you. Alcie brushes me off, and you brush Peter. What do you think you're doing?"

"Why, nothing. We. . . ."

"I don't blame Alcie," he rushed on, without letting her finish. "She wants to get married, but quick, so Jon's her man. I'll have a long, gray beard before I get around to it. But *you!* Gee whizz, you're supposed to have some sense."

"Bobby, I don't want to start an argument. I didn't hunt you up," Tippy pointed out with dignity, "you hunted me. I'll have to live my life the way I think it's best for me—not for you, or even Peter."

"Okay." He brushed a pebble with the toe of his shoe and seemed to relent. His eyes were on the ground and the stone he pushed around, and he finally admitted, "I like Ken all right, if he's the one you want. And I guess Pete will make out. He has his New York gal to fall back on."

"Maxsie?" Tippy took the bait even though she didn't mean to. Maxsie Green, black of hair and sophisticate *de luxe,* had come up to dances with Peter while Tippy was in Europe. "Does—does he date her now?" she asked, and hated herself for wanting to know.

"I saw her around last week. They were in the Boodlers together."

"Oh."

Bobby had done what he could for Peter. He gave the pebble a kick that sent it hopping over the finer gravel and prepared for departure by asking, "Where'll I pick up my cake?"

"I'll leave it with the guard in Grant Hall." Tippy studied him carefully as he pulled his blouse down in front and reached around to rub the back. "You're really sweet, Bobby," she said, helping him brush away the dust from the wall. "Peter's lucky to have you for a friend."

"I do what I can."

"Even to trying to make me jealous. Well," she gave his thin shoulders a final pat and admitted, "I did feel a twinge—but just a twinge. I hope Peter *will* see Maxsie. Would you like to drive back with us?"

"I wouldn't mind."

She thought of that conversation while her parents went off into their own discussion of Bobby's precarious academic footing, and said with a grin, "I wouldn't worry about him. What he lacks in brains he has in brass. If he can't handle a subject he'll twist it around till no one else can either. He knows the answers—and they're all his own."

She smiled a little as she went upstairs, an amused, tolerant smile for Bobby and an annoyed smile for the damage he had done. Maxsie's image, once called to mind, had made the rest of her date almost a threesome.

"*It wasn't fair,*" she wrote to Ken, without even waiting to take off her coat, "*for Peter, I mean. He asked me up next week end and was darling to me, but I don't think I should go again. Really, I don't, darling. I don't want Peter. I just want you. So I think I should give him a chance to find someone else. I turned down any more dates with him because—oh, Ken, no one matters but you.*"

The following days were dull, with nothing to look forward to. Peter still telephoned at regular intervals and went off on his football trips. He argued that she should come up to a dance but she always found herself too busy. Her excuses sounded fine over the telephone, the parties she described. Some were in town, some at Briarcliff; and she wished she actually could go to all the gay, imaginary week ends she talked about.

Tippy knew very few of the girls at school. As a day pupil, she threw her books in her car when classes were over and hurried home. Most of the students lived in the sprawling dormitories and went chattering up to their rooms, full of their own plans and engagements.

There was one she wished she could know. Her name was Theodosia Brant, and she reminded Tippy of Alice. Not that she looked like Alice, for she wasn't even pretty. Her hair was a mousy brown with a bad permanent, too short and fuzzy, and she had a large mouth, a decided nose, and blue eyes. But she talked like Alice. She had a way of standing sturdily and making a forthright reply that caught the class's attention. When she knew the answer to a question, she gave it, and when she didn't, she simply said, "I'm sorry, I don't know," in a way that was a delightful change from everybody else's floundering.

Since Briarcliff wasn't an expensive school and the girls all said Theodosia was "rolling in money" and let her alone, she seemed to be a happy misfit. Tippy liked her. She wondered about her. Having plenty of time to wonder about anything and anyone, she spent it on Theodosia Brant. Why did she choose Briarcliff? Why was she so happy there, going off on whistling walks alone, wearing ugly, baggy sweaters, and never trying to improve her looks or her discouraging hair?

Tippy considered Theodosia on her trips to and from school. She sometimes wondered what her interest could be in such an uninteresting person, and asked herself, "Why should I want to know her? She's sort of like Alcie, yes; but I have Alcie. I can be with her whenever I want to and I don't think I'd even enjoy Theo much." But the idea persisted and she moved to Theodosia's table at lunch and sent a shy smile across to her.

The smile was met with a warm, generous one. It spread like a glow and made Tippy lean across the table to ask, "How about driving home with me after school and having dinner? We'll bring you back."

She suddenly knew what she wanted of Theodosia. She wanted her for Bobby. She had found him another Alice. It amused her to do something kind for her inconsiderate brother, to bring joy into his dull life, and she felt virtuous and pleased with herself. It didn't occur to her that Bobby might resent it.

The full impact of that struck her after she and her happy guest had spent a whole evening learning facts about each other. Theodosia's room at school held no photographs of living human beings; and seeing that before they started out, it took skill and tact for Tippy to learn anything at all about her.

"Hello, Bobby," she said, making a prompt telephone call after her father had put on his overcoat and gone to drive eight miles in the cold. "How would you like a date for Saturday night?"

"I wouldn't," came the prompt reply.

"With a swell gal, Bob." Tippy intentionally discarded his hated nickname, and waited.

"No, thanks."

"But you have to!" And she resorted to wailing, "I've already told her you'd ask her. I promised her. She's lonesome, she's rich. She hasn't any parents—just a guardian who pushes her off any old place and sent her to Briarcliff."

"If she goes to that school, the answer is no. You've told me enough and I have to study now."

"But, Bobby, please," Tippy pleaded. "She's a lot like Alcie. I simply found her for you because she reminds me of Alcie."

"Then the answer is double no. Alcie done me wrong."

A loud sigh that was much too hearty to sound convincing bounced against Tippy's ear and she knew the demon on the other end of the line was grinning. "Oh, listen, Bobby," she humbled herself to plead, "I never ask you to do favors for me. I carry cakes up to you and I tried to cheer you up last year when you were so worried about your grades, and I never hang around and bother you. One date couldn't hurt you. You can make all your classmates dance with her if you want to. She's rich." This seemed an unfair argument to use for a friend, but she repeated desperately, "She's rich. She has a car."

"What did you say her name is?"

"I didn't say; but it's Theodosia Brant. We call her Theo."

Progress was being made for Bobby's sigh was genuine this time. "Oh, gosh, Tip," he said unhappily, "I don't want to drag her."

"You will when you know her." Tippy silently vowed to do something about Theodosia's hair. "She's not beautiful," she added, just in case it would be safer to have that statement on the record, "but she's sweet and nice, and —a grand gal."

"I can hardly wait."

"And she thinks you're the handsomest thing she ever saw. I almost gave her your picture to take home with her."

"Do, and I'll autograph it." There was a long pause before he asked despondently, "Do I have to drag up a date for you, too?"

"Oh, I'm not coming." Tippy was full of laughter and bright remarks before she rushed downstairs to tell her mother what she had accomplished.

"I know he'll like Theo," she gloated, "if he'll only put his mind to it. He liked Alcie."

"But, darling." Mrs. Parrish thought Tippy really was in a sad way when she must find her pleasure in doing for Bobby, and she suggested, "Why don't you go, too? Bobby fusses but he'd love to get a date for you. He'd be very proud to have his sister at one of his dances, and you've never gone."

"His class is too young." Tippy folded her hands in her lap and said, matching her thumbnails together, "I know I'm only eighteen and he's almost twenty-one, but after you're used to being with an officer like Ken, or even with Peter who'll graduate in June, third classmen seem such juveniles. Bobby's crowd is so silly."

"I don't think so. Alcie didn't. Penny went around with David's friends, and she was nearer his age than you are Bobby's." Mrs. Parrish sighed and adjusted the lamp beside her. It's glow touched Tippy's small, lonely face, and she urged, "Go up to the dance, darling, or to Peter's. He wants you to come."

It was almost time for Peter's Wednesday night call and Tippy got up slowly. "I want to write to Ken," she said. "If Alcie doesn't have the Princeton bunch up as she sort of planned, I'll go to the Point."

"Promise?"

"I promise."

She rubbed her cheek against her mother's and was careful to hum as she went up the stairway, loud enough to carry back to the living room. Poor dears, she thought dolefully, turning on her desk lamp and taking Ken's precious packet of letters from a little drawer in her bedside table, they do worry about me. Penny was always so busy and full of fun. I must be an awful trial to them. Well, I'm me, and that's the way I am.

She did go down to Governors Island and Alice's party, after all. Friday afternoon was spent with Theodosia, deciding on one of her surprisingly beautiful evening gowns and setting her hair. Then Tippy drove to New York.

One thing more to write about to Ken—her whirl of silly good times. She wondered where he was, if he had a room to sleep in or only the sky and bursting shells for a roof. Was he muddy and cold in a jeep while her little heater hummed? Was he fighting now or lying in exhausted sleep? It was yesterday wherever he was. He had lost one of his precious days while he traveled and she had lived a whole day longer than he.

"When he comes back," she sat up straighter to tell herself in the windshield mirror, "he'll pick it up again. That day will belong to me. We'll pick it up together—right in San Francisco, I betcha."

The party, in spite of her reluctance to go, was fun. She envied Alice her big Jonathan Drayton. Alice's smile was so confident, her eyes so serene, and her future so perfectly planned, that Tippy asked when the guests had left, "What would you do if Jon should be drafted?"

Alice sat down on a sofa and stared up at her. Her smile was gone but her eyes were still a clear, cool gray as she answered, "Why, he'd have to go. I've expected him to, Tippy, because he's had his R.O.T.C. in college. But things in Korea look so much better now that I'm hoping he won't have to. We're pushing the Communists back behind the thirty-eighth parallel," she pointed out. "Why?"

"Would you marry him?"

"Yes." Alice's smile came back and she said slyly, "Jon and I think things should be settled one way or another by June."

"June?" It was Tippy's turn to stare. "I thought you said *September!*" she cried, letting cigarette stubs spill out of the ash tray she was about to empty into the fireplace.

"We think we can do it by June. Jon's going into advertising with his father and I had a talk with Daddy." Alice drew up her knees and patted the cushion beside her. "Sit down and let me tell you," she coaxed. "I've been dying to all evening, because we just decided yesterday. You know the house Jon's parents are letting us live in?" she asked, as Tippy perched on the edge of the sofa and mutely nodded. "Well, that and an allowance from my

Gwen + Alcie's father's estate

Mother is mother of all Jordons except Jennifer + Peter

mother's estate will let us do it. Jon's salary will be practically nothing at first, but we can buy some furniture and beg a lot more, and Daddy thinks I should have the same allowance from my money that he sends to Gwenn in Hollywood. You know," she said, "I've never thought about having a different father from all the rest of the Jordons. Daddy has always been my father. And it seems strange that a man who died right after I was born could leave all this money to Mother, for Gwenn and me. It doesn't seem fair, but I'm glad to have it right now. And," she leaned forward to say with shining eyes, "I want you to be my maid of honor."

"Oh, Alcie, I'm so happy for you." Tippy leaned back in complete repose and satisfaction. "I've been so jealous all evening," she confessed, "of the way Jon hovers over you and waits on you, but I'm thrilled now. It was nasty of me to bring up the war."

"No, it wasn't, Tip. I hate to think of what I'd be like in your place. You see," she said carefully, "I do have Jon. It's easy to plan for something that's way off in the future and may never happen at all. Jon may never have to go; and if he should, I can close up the house and tag along. And that reminds me of another thing I wanted to tell you. Daddy's due for overseas. He's sure he'll have to go this summer so that's another reason why we pushed my wedding up."

She paused for breath and Tippy asked, "What will you do with all the children?"

"Oh, we'll manage." Alice laughed because she was accustomed to including all the rest of the Jordons in whatever she did. "Jenifer and Cyril are coming back from

England for the summer, but they'll keep the two they have, and Daddy'll rent a house near me and put the others in it when he has to leave. Ellin mothered us all through the last war and she has poor dopey Rosie to help her; and if anything goes wrong, I'll be near enough to take charge."

"Won't Gwenn help you out?"

"From Hollywood?" Alice laughed and said, "Susan thinks it would be wonderful to go out and stay with Gwenn, but I'd hate to see her after a week of it. As far as I can make out, Gwenn exists on a diet of lettuce. Party food followed by lettuce. And now, let's talk about my wedding. What colors shall we have?"

It was late Sunday afternoon when Tippy drove home. She was a little tired from living on other peoples' happiness. Alice had presented her with the whole wedding, as much as to say, "There, that will give you something to do"; and she was placid and agreeable to any suggestions. Tippy was to select the bridesmaids' dresses. She was also to aid the bride in her own choice and plan the decorations for the old stone chapel.

Then there was Theodosia. If Alice and her affairs didn't fill up enough of the time that had to pass between now and a year from Christmas, there was Theodosia in the offing. She would either rave over a week end with the army's pride and joy or never speak to Tippy again. "All in all," Tippy sighed, opening the front door and receiving Switzy's bounces, "I'm busier than a one-armed paper hanger with a mosquito on his neck."

Switzy wore a note tied to his collar and she tried to hold him still so she could pull it off and read it. She finally did, and it said, *"Have all gone to David's. He has his or-ders. Come over. There's a letter for you on the mantel."*

"Well, what do you know?" she asked him, and let him hang across her hip while she went to get her letter, and sit on her lap while she read it.

He curled contentedly against her until she began tak-ing in happy gulps of air and turned pages with excited jerks that dug him with her elbow. Then he got down and returned to his favorite place by the door.

"Listen, you silly little dog," she called, shaking the letter at him. "Don't you want to hear what Ken says?"

Switzy gave his pompon a wag and rolled over on his back with his tongue hanging comfortably out, but she jumped up and began to read to him anyway. She stood in the middle of the living room and read like a district attorney addressing the jury. *"I'm way up yonder. If you follow the papers you may know where it is, but we're going so fast I can't keep up with myself. General Mac-Arthur has given us the slogan 'Home by Christmas,' and the men are putting everything they have into the march. Oh, cherub, darling. . . ."* Tippy broke off and looked down. "You don't need to listen to the rest," she said. "It's just for me." Then she caught him up and began to whirl him around.

He hung like a limp puppet, whining dizzily, until she kissed his topknot and let him drop. "I think we'd better go tell David he can take off his uniform!" she cried, and raced him to the door.

CHAPTER VIII

TIPPY ALWAYS enjoyed going to Gladstone. She had once remarked to Penny, "It pleasures me to have rich relatives." And while Penny's long, white house was old and beautiful, Gladstone was truly an estate.

The mansion was set in a vast park, complete with a high, protective wall and a lodge house. Usually Tippy savored her stately arrival, but on this late October evening she was so full of her good news that she beat out the family signal on her horn and swung past the little cottage and along the winding road that led to a mass of brick and turrets. A twist of her wheel brought her around a fountain before a stone terrace and spilled Switzy off the seat. Lights shone out from tall French windows beyond the terrace, and she flung open the car door and ran up a shallow flight of steps.

"Now you be a good dog," she took time to admonish before she banged open a great oak door that could have withstood a battering ram. "Don't fuss with your cousins, even though they're horrid beasts and growl at you."

Perkins, the English butler, hurried out of his little office which overlooked the driveway, full of apologies for having missed her entrance. But he could only take the beaver coat she pushed at him, hear her say, "Oh, thanks, I'm in a fearful rush," and watch her skid across the Oriental rugs, into the long, formal drawing room.

"I bear news!" she cried, waving the letter she had

clutched all the way. "You can all relax. The war is practically over!"

Everyone in the separate groups sat up to stare at her.
David, looking most unlike himself in olive drab, left the
mantel he was leaning against and asked, "Has something
new come in over the radio, Tip?"

She was the center of their attention. Josh stopped with
a sentence unfinished, Penny left little Parri with her foot
on the sofa and her shoe half-tied, while Tippy said importantly, "I have a letter from Ken. He'll be home for
Christmas and I won't have to send him a package! General MacArthur says so."

"Oh, cherub!" Penny went back to tying Parri's shoe
and stopped her hopping for balance. "We've known we
were winning," she said above the others, "and so did
you."

"But *Ken* told me."

Tippy was embarrassed now, as she watched her beautiful sister-in-law come toward her. Carrol, she thought,
should have more to rejoice about than anyone, yet her
lovely face was quiet. She never teased as Penny did, and
she said gently now, "It *is* good news, darling. If Ken
says it, and he's over there where he should know, it lifts
a load off my heart. Have you had your dinner?"

"Not yet." Tippy watched Penny finish Parri's white
shoe and give her a gentle push back to the library and
the other children. "You don't really think he'll be home,
do you?" she asked the room in general.

"Not quite that soon, Tippy," Josh answered. His
rugged, homely face smiled at her as he tapped his pipe
out on the brass fire screen, and he said, "We've all been

discussing the way the whole thing has blown wide open
—but Ken's regular army, you know. The boys will be
pulled out all right, but I think he'll be left to finish his
tour. Perhaps in Japan. Did he say he might be home?"

"No, he didn't say that."

Tippy wished she hadn't been so dramatic. Had Bobby
made such an error, he would bluff his way out by con-
tending Ken had said it and was due any day, and Penny
would have continued flinging joy around like rose petals.
She could only change the subject by saying in a small
voice, "You look nice, David."

"Think so?" David gave her his full military bearing
and said proudly, "After almost six years in moth balls not
a seam had to be changed. Come on in, Tip, and liven us
up some more."

"I feel—sort of silly," she gulped, and was glad David's
young pointer chose that moment to crawl out from behind a sofa and start a fight.

Switzy's surprised yelp and the scramble it caused gave
her a chance to become just any member of the family
again. The pointer was banished, Switzy was comforted
with a piece of candy, and Penny pulled her down beside
her. "I'm sorry I was so clumsy about Ken," she said.
"Don't stop hoping, pet, because he *may* come home. I'd
want to murder anyone who knocked the props out from
under me like that."

"It's all right. I've been following the war the same as
the rest of you have," Tippy explained, trying to justify
herself. "I know all about Seoul and crossing the thirty-
eighth parallel." She leaned closer and asked, in a voice

as apologetic as Penny's had been, "Where is David going? I forgot to say anything to him about it."

"Out to Knox. He and Carrol are leaving tomorrow and they'll send for the children as soon as they find a house."

"Do lieutenant colonels rank houses on the post?"

"He hopes so. If not, they'll rent a place somewhere."

Perkins returned to announce with the formality Carrol's father had always required and which she could never make him change, "Dinner is served, madam"; and the room became active again.

All the family—parents, children and grandchildren —sat at a long dining-room table and watched David carve a turkey. Little Davy had a chair like the others, Lang, a matching one that was only a little higher, and the two little MacDonalds were lifted onto fat dictionaries, topped by as many pillows as were needed to bring Joshu's black head above the table.

"Just like all our wonderful times," Mrs. Parrish said, completely contented for this one evening, "except, as usual, Bobby is missing. I did want you to tell him good-by, David."

"I saw him this morning," David answered, severing a wing from the turkey and trying to see around the platter Perkins slid under it. "Just set that plate down, I'll find it. Carrol and I drove up to the Academy and went to chapel. I looked around for our young friend, and out he comes with a girl. Not Alcie," he said with amazement, "a strange one. Not bad, either."

"She was very attractive," Carrol added, pushing Lang's hand away from her butter plate and trying to wake up Joshu. "Serve the children first tonight, David."

"Was he—nice to her?" Tippy asked, afraid to hear the verdict.

"Seemed to be. Said he was taking her to the Thayer for lunch."

David motioned Perkins along the line with a filled plate by pointing his carving knife at the sleepiest head; and Colonel Parrish remarked dryly, "If he passes up a free meal and parts with any money for one, she's doing all right. She's a friend of Tippy's at school."

Conversation turned to Briarcliff, and Tippy was relieved to know it was safe to return there. Her brother had not disgraced her. She was also happy to know he wouldn't demand a pound of her flesh for a ruined week end.

The after-dinner lingering was short because of sleepy children, and when her parents left in their car, she and Switzy trailed them in the little coupé that belonged to her now.

David had taken her aside and said, "Keep your chin up, honey. This whole business will be over soon, and we'll be throwing you a wedding. You can have the little car you've been using if you want it." Then he had bent down to pat Tippy's faithful escort, Switzy, and pay him a great compliment by telling him, "You're a darned nice little dog. You're a real gentleman."

Tippy impressed that on Switzy as they rode along and proudly wrote it to Ken when she was alone in her room. The world was a beautiful place. It was so full of hope and good fortune that when Peter telephoned for a chat, she found herself exclaiming, "I'd *love* to come up next week!"

Even upsetting Peter's life didn't seem to matter so

much now, for this state of affairs wouldn't go on much longer. Ken would come home. Peter would graduate and go off and forget—and *Ken would come home.*

Tippy sang through the following weeks. November was a gala month. It was marked, not by the dances she went to or the football game she saw at Princeton with Alice, Jonathan, and one of his fraternity brothers, not even by Bobby's condescending kindness or Theodosia's grateful blossoming, but by the pins she stuck in a map.

Colonel Parrish kept a large map of Korea on the wall of his upstairs sitting room. He liked to watch the strategy of field commanders, planning his own moves and checking each maneuver with theirs to see how right he had been. It was his morning's entertainment until Tippy took charge of the pins. She pushed each blue pin in with a pat and gave the retreating red ones a whack with her thumb. Finally, the pins went so high she had to stand on tiptoe to reach them.

"Home by Christmas" was a song in her heart. Even should Ken stay on, other boys would be home. Christmas trees would bloom. And she sang while she punched in her pins, "May your days be merry and bright—and may all your Christmases be white."

She bought gifts for Ken and worried because they had to fit into such a little box. It was the regulation size, just large enough to hold a pair of fur lined gloves, a pair of crooked socks she had knitted, a leather-framed snapshot of the two of them in Germany, and a gold identification bracelet. At the last minute she squeezed in a white candle angel, trimmed with gold tinsel. *"So you can light it,"* she scribbled on the card, *"and remember the way you*

said I looked in Germany—like a Christmas tree angel."
And she sent her white dress with the gold embroidery to
the cleaner, ready to wear on Christmas day.

Oh, November was a wonderful month. People went
about grinning and saying cheerily, "It won't be long
now." Thankful prayers were said in homes and churches,
and even the President and the Secretary of War came in
for some praise. Peter and his classmates fumed because
they would miss the show. Too young for one war, this one
would be over before they could pitch their diplomas into
their foot lockers, put on their new uniforms, and go charging off to battle. "Darn it," they grumbled while they
danced, "the army'll be back to counting beans by June."

And then, on November twenty-sixth, the whole world
rocked.

Two hundred thousand Chinese Communists poured
down through Manchuria. United Nation's forces were
slaughtered; American marines were trapped; the Seventh
Infantry was caught in the Changjin reservoir; Seoul was
cut off. The old war was over, and General MacArthur
announced that a new one had begun.

Tippy stood with her pins that morning and didn't
know where to put them. She simply left them lying on her
father's desk through fourteen days of furious fighting.
Blue pins and red lay jumbled together and were indica-
tive of the forces locked in struggle.

A letter came from Ken. It was still sanguine and full of
plans for at least a short leave—and had been written
two weeks before the onslaught. A second one was just
a hurried scrawl, then there was silence.

Tippy couldn't know that Ken had taken his precious

rest hour to scribble that last note; that grimy, aching from fatigue and cold, he had sat in a bombed hut with its windows out, its roof blown off, holding a cup of hot coffee in his hands to warm his stiff fingers enough to hold a pencil. The letter was brief because he had a second one to write.

It simply said he loved her, that he was fine and looking forward to coming home. It was all he could think of to say. It was what he wanted to say and prayed would come true; and he licked the flap and pressed it flat, then hunched himself higher against the cold stone wall and hunted through his worn dispatch case for another piece of paper.

This letter was harder to write. Several times he stopped and sat listening to the steady boom of guns, the whirr of a plane streaking overhead, rough, cheerful voices in the chow line outside. The little spray of hair Tippy loved was mashed into the mat under his steel helmet and his trench-coat sleeve was smeared with dirt it had wiped from his face. Even his eyes were drooping from exhaustion and not the sleepy slant nature had given them, and he pushed his pencil wearily back and forth across the page.

"Hey, Ken," a voice called from outside, and he dragged his head up. "It's time to go."

"Just a minute." There were a few more lines he must add, and he scribbled them as fast as he could.

"The old man's yelling for you."

A gaunt face poked through the glassless window as another tired young officer set a pair of field glasses inside and said, "Here, these are yours. We've got to get under way while the artillery can still give us some cover fire."

"I'm coming."

Ken scrawled his signature and shoved the letter into another envelope. There was no time to reread what he had written. The thunder of guns was louder now, the retreating columns not so orderly. Planes gave some protection, big guns boomed from behind and delayed the enemy, but every man on this besieged hill was protecting his own life as best he could. A whole regiment was on the run. He wrote Tippy's name again and held his pencil over the envelope.

"Ken?"

"TO BE MAILED IN THE EVENT OF MY DEATH," he printed firmly, and crammed the letter into his case beside its mate. "Okay, Stevens," he yelled, and crawled wearily to his feet.

Tippy only knew that no more letters came. The short, scribbled note was the last.

"Darling, why don't you go somewhere?" her mother urged, watching her wait forlornly in the window seat for the postman.

"I don't know anywhere to go."

"Well, shopping with Alcie," she suggested. "Do Christmas shopping."

"Alcie's always buying something for her trousseau, now, and I don't seem to care about Christmas. People all look so glum in the stores."

"Then drive in with Penny and see her play again. She loves to have you."

"For the fifty-second time? No, thanks." Tippy left the window and shook her head. "Don't worry about me," she said. "Poor dear, you keep pointing out to me that we're getting most of our troops back to Hungnam for evacuation, and I know we are. I know we'll get them out, just as well as you do. America always manages somehow, but I want a letter. I hate to go two inches away for fear I'll miss it."

"A few hours wouldn't matter and the postman's always late. Go up and see Bobby. Skip school tomorrow and go up and see him."

Tippy laughed at that suggestion. "You are at the end of your wits," she said. "If I'm feeling low now, five minutes with Robert would finish me. If you really want me out of your way so much, I'll go for a drive. It's free hour up at the Point, and I'll drive up and see Peter."

She didn't know why she decided on Peter as a choice, except that his rumbling bass had been a comfort to her. It was he, far more than the news commentators, who kept her hopeful that the American navy would evacuate the trapped United Nation's forces. He explained the situation in words Tippy could understand and showed her how it could be done. He was so matter-of-fact in his reasoning that she had come to depend on his calls that were nightly now, and waited for them as a prisoner waits for a guard to bring his evening meal. "I guess I'll go see Peter," she repeated.

"Do," her mother urged; and Tippy knew what peace and relief she left behind her.

She drove slowly along the familiar road, not knowing exactly what she wanted to do. She simply was removing herself from troubled anxiety at home. Looking for Peter in his usual haunts seemed a useless waste of effort, and she decided to ride around West Point like a tourist, and let anything happen.

The United States Military Academy, even on a cold December day, is always interesting; and she drove up and down its winding roads, looking at its officers' quarters and buildings, the square of stone barracks that housed its corps of cadets. The busy cadets themselves hurried along in their heavy gray overcoats, little whiffs of breath popping from their mouths like steam through the exhausts of working motors; and every now and then a fourth classman trotted along at a faster pace than the others, puffing like an overheated boiler. Tippy smiled whenever she saw one and tried to imagine what Ken had been like as a plebe, scurrying through his day and afraid to loiter.

Peter was not to be seen. He was in the Boodlers, exactly where she had decided not to look, and he was sitting at a table with Bobby.

He had been on his way back to barracks from a late class when Bobby had loomed up on the sidewalk outside Grant Hall. "Hi," Peter said, stopping him. "What's the rush?"

"I may have a date," Bobby puffed, "don't know yet. Where are you going?"

"Nowhere. Want to go along?"

"Don't mind if I do. Have you any ideas where it'll be?"

Peter grinned and considered. Should a date show up for Bobby it was bound to be here, so he asked, "Boodle?" and Bobby nodded. "I hear you have a new drag," he went on, as they took the stone steps in stride.

"Yep." Bobby nodded again. "Friend of Tippy's," he said magnanimously. "I just tow her around."

Whenever Bobby "towed anyone around" from pure generosity, little wings would sprout on his shoulders and a golden nimbus encircle his head. No feathers stuck through the cape on his overcoat and no halo ringed the cap he tossed on one of the sturdy oak chairs in the Boodlers; and Peter said, "You don't fool me. I saw her cream convertible and her top-notch clothes. What will you have?"

"Something 'gooey.'" Bobby plopped himself into a chair beside his cap and considered the Boodlers' limited menu. "I guess a chocolate nut sundae," he decided after hungry deliberation. "With whipped cream on top. Want some tickets?"

"I have some."

Peter took his book of checks from his cap and went over to the counter to give their order. When he came back with Bobby's sundae and a glass of root beer for himself, he pulled another chair into place with his foot and sat down to ask, "Have you seen Tip lately?"

"Not much. Theo—that's the *femme*—tells me she's getting around a lot. Other sources say she's coming up with you again."

"Not enough. I talk with her almost every night, though."

"Why?" Bobby stopped smearing his sundae into a mess and looked up. His eyes were round and blue, and they bored into Peter's level gaze like diamonds cutting through glass. "What do you get out of it?" he wanted to know. "Tippy's gone, finished, pffft. Why hang around?"

"Because she's still Tippy." Peter's voice was low and sure. "I know she's in love with Prescott," he said. "I'm going to have a long, lonely life ahead of me when I leave here. These few months mean a lot."

"I can't see it." Bobby returned to his ice cream, then laid his spoon down again and said with unusual understanding, "Listen, Pete. It doesn't do any good to keep on banging your heart against a stone wall. You only put more bruises on it. Let it heal. Find yourself another *femme*—they're everywhere, if you'll only look around."

"I guess I don't want to." Peter reached for the package of cigarettes he had kept in his cap since the end of football season, and said while he pulled one out and struck a match, "I don't even see them."

"Not Maxsie Green?"

"Nope."

"Gosh." Chocolate dripped over the glass and spread in a little puddle on the table while Bobby watched it. "I may have done you wrong," he said uncomfortably, "but I saw her up here one afternoon and told Tip about it."

"It wouldn't matter. She just drove up with some friends and I bought her a drink."

"But Tip was mad." Bobby ruffled his short, curly thatch and repeated with wonder, "She was kind of mad. Do you think it could mean anything?"

"No, I wish I did, but I don't. Not unless it made her decide, just as you have, that she ought to let me alone. She did, for a while. It didn't do much good and I still didn't hunt up any other girls so she's been coming up again." Peter crossed his arms on the table and leaned forward as he said, "I've been wanting to have a talk with you like this. Sometimes . . ." he looked down at the smoke curling up from his fingers . . . "sometimes I think I can't take it. I feel as if there's got to be *something* I can do. There isn't. There isn't one darn thing. I get to feeling sorry for myself, even while I want Tippy to be happy. She is, don't you think?"

"Yeah. I wish Ken weren't a decent Joe." Sympathy lay heavy on Bobby but it seemed a shame to waste a good sundae, so he pulled the glass closer and bent over it. He bolted it down and said when he finished, just as if there had been no time pause, "I want Tippy happy, too. That sounds crazy coming from me, but I do. She's always been a nice little kid and I tease her because it's fun. Pen always bats things off, but Tip's the kind they hurt, I know they do. She's not happy, Pete, over this setup."

"I want her to be. She's worried sick over the turn the war's taken, and so whatever I say to you let's keep between ourselves. Be nice to her, will you?"

"I am. I've been darned good to her lately. I've got her thinking of me as a—brother."

"So have I. Well, brother," Peter stubbed out his cigarette and stood up, "having settled our sister's future by letting her keep the guy she's going to keep anyway, let's adjourn. Are you heading for barracks?"

"Not yet. I'll sit a bit and see if Theo shows up."

Three cadets stormed in with loud calls for service, and as he got up to join them, Bobby laid a hand on Peter's shoulder. "Don't let it get you down, Pete," he counciled. "Girls aren't worth it, believe me."

"No?" Peter grinned as he buttoned up his overcoat. "You don't believe that, you dope."

"Pete." Bobby's hand shot out. It was the only way he could show his respect and liking. It was the way a good upper classman gave lowly plebes a lift. It was West Point's way of extending friendship.

"Thanks, Bob." Peter grasped the hand. "Thanks," he said huskily, and went out into the early dusk.

A car was going slowly past, and he stood on the steps to watch it. It was a little black car with a familiar license number; and he watched it roll slowly along the street and turn the corner

CHAPTER IX

"DARLING, there will surely be a letter tomorrow, so stop worrying," Mrs. Parrish coaxed.

So many days had passed since the evacuation had been accomplished. Even Christmas was gone. Several letters had come from Ken, but they had all been old ones that had wandered around or lain in some overseas post office. There had been a Christmas box, too, smashed and with its wrapping paper torn, its clumsily tied packages spilling out their contents: a lovely string of cultured pearls, ordered from Japan; a gaudy silk scarf, product of a post exchange; and bits of gold and glass that might have been a pin.

Tippy had fingered everything, over and over; and when she clasped the necklace around her throat, she looked at herself in the mirror and quoted, " 'The bride wore pearls, gift of the groom.' "

Then came silence again, until even Colonel and Mrs. Parrish were afraid to meet each new day, and began cautious inquiries through the Pentagon. No one could find Ken's name on a casualty list, and Mrs. Parrish dared say, "Don't you see, darling? Everything's all right. Ken's probably on a ship somewhere. He's being moved. He can't write to you, honey."

"I hope that's it. My goodness, it's been a whole month."

The new year had begun. January was cold and blustery. Snow plows did their ceaseless best to keep the roads

clear, but they left icy patches that made driving hazard-
ous. Tippy crawled to school in her car that wore clanking
chains for bracelets; and when the sky split open one afternoon and tossed out a white goose-down quilt, she found
herself marooned there. She was in a whipped-cream
world, as cut off from home as Ken was. Wires went down,
lights flickered out, and a hundred and fifty girls braved
the stinging snow to pelt each other and exercise their
muscles.

Tippy felt silly. She felt as nonsensical as Parri when
she put on a red snow suit of Theodosia's and one of her
baggy sweaters that looked like fifty cents but had a price
tag of fifteen dollars still on it. But she pelted away as
hard as any of the others, and found herself made captain of a backslapping team that vanquished other groups
and sent them stamping inside for dry clothes.

She was glad the telephone wires had clung to their
poles until after she had called home. The school had
turned an unavoidable situation into a holiday, and the
college wing of the dormitory was making merry. Flash-
lights flickered along the corridors like fireflies, and there
were constant shouts of, "Look out, dope, that's not a door
—it's me"; "Feel around on the floor if you can't find the
candy"; or "Come down to my room, I have a candle."

By eight o'clock lanterns had been brought from a
storeroom, filled and hung in enough strategic places to
stop the enjoyable game of blindman's buff, and a meal of
sorts was served in the vast, dim dining room. Tippy sat
on Theodosia's bed and munched cheese and crackers
instead, feeling for slabs of bologna Theodosia hacked

off with a penknife. It was cozy, and she was having her first taste of real college life.

"I have a date with Bobby tomorrow night," Theodosia said, stumbling around for the milk bottle she had brought up on her last foray on the kitchens. "My chances aren't much for making it. Have some pie."

She had gathered together quite a meal, and Tippy wondered how she had done it. Probably with money, she thought comfortably. Money could do a lot, for Theodosia was saying, "I know a man who owns a horse and sleigh he'll rent me. He could drive us up to the dance and come back and get us."

"In this storm?" Even money couldn't stop the heavens from dumping snow when they had too much in their storage clouds; and Tippy said, "No man in his right mind would let a horse go out in this. If it clears up tomorrow, I'd rather take a chance on my car with chains."

"You couldn't do it." Theodosia sat in the dark and considered conditions. "I'm not one for risking my neck," she decided, "but I do want to go to that dance. I'm going social in such a big way and have dug up drags for so many girls that I'm almost president of a lonely hearts club. I can't let my followers down, so I think I'd better rent that horse. I wrote the man's name down somewhere."

She struck a match and flipped through pages in an address book, until Tippy reminded, "The phone's gone off. Have you forgotten that little hitch?"

"It'll come on. The telephone company prides itself on its service. And if it doesn't, I'll borrow Meg Marston's snowshoes and mush over to the farm. Ah, here he is. Mr. Clem Crane."

"What's the horse's name?" Tippy asked idly.

"Annex."

"For goodness' sake, how do you know?"

"I fed him and asked Mr. Crane. That was before I knew you," Theodosia said, through the dark again. "I was sort of lonely and I wandered in there and thought I might like to go jingling around this winter. We use sleighs a lot in Vermont," she explained. "He said I could have Annex whenever I want him."

The match flared again and went toward the closet, and Tippy followed its path. She thought Theo quite capable of setting out for Mr. Crane's tonight, just to make sure she would have a horse tomorrow, and asked with interest, "You aren't going *now*, are you?"

"I'm looking for my fur-lined gloves. Ouch. That burned."

Going to West Point in a sleigh began to sound like fun. So far as Tippy knew, no one ever had arrived in such a manner, and she lay back to contemplate it. She and Ken had ridden in sleighs, in Switzerland. In cold, frosty air, under a mountain of bear robes. They had gone swooping down white ski runs and had climbed into sleighs and been comfortably driven back to their hotel. Her thoughts always seemed to return to Ken, and she pushed them aside when fur tickled her face and Theodosia said, "Smell the moth balls. Good, huh?"

The lights flashed on in a sudden blaze, and Tippy was surprised to find herself looking, not at gloves, but at a coonskin cap.

"That was my daddy's," Theodosia said, blinking. "He was in the lumber business, and we always kept a hunting lodge, way up in Maine. When I was a little kid, I had a cap, too." She broke off and smoothed the fur tenderly. "I shot the coon for mine and dressed it, all by myself."

"You had a nice childhood, Theo, didn't you?"

"Yep, and I'm glad I can remember it."

"But you haven't any pictures." Tippy paused, then said resolutely, "Of your parents. Why not?"

"Pictures hurt you. They're just reminders of something that's better to forget. I have lots of them, but I don't keep them around for people to stare at or to stare at myself."

Tippy turned her eyes to Theodosia's dresser that now held a photograph of Bobby, looking too sweet and good to be true; and watching her, Theodosia said quickly, "Bob's alive. He's in my life right now."

"And if anything happened and he wasn't, you'd put the picture away?"

"Sure I would. It's like this, Tippy," she sat on the foot of the bed to say, "My daddy always told me, 'Don't keep sticking pins in yourself so you'll go on suffering. If something hurts you, forget it, go on.' It hurts me to look at his picture, but to remember the good times we had together, doesn't. It's the same way with Mom—so I don't have the pictures. I do a lot better without them."

It was a new philosophy to Tippy, and a strange one. The Parrishes lived with their family photographs. They needed them. But, she suddenly reasoned, all the subjects were alive. There was no hurting ache when they smiled from their frames.

"I don't know if I could feel that way," she said. It seems to fit your disposition. But for me? I don't know."

"I hope you never have to find out."

Theodosia began choosing a dress for Tippy to wear to the dance. The wind stopped, the snow drifted down like flour from a sifter that was almost empty, and toward morning a timid moon peeked out. Theodosia was up early and off after her horse.

"My goodness, I don't know what your parents would think," Miss Tremaine, the principal of the school, worried at eleven o'clock, standing in the portico of the main building and protecting her nose and mouth with a scarf. "Such foolishness."

"But fun," Tippy answered, as she and three other girls in snow suits pushed through a gathering of envious onlookers.

In spite of the cold, heads hung from most of the open windows in the old brick building. Someone yelled, "Whoa, Dobbin," and the rough-coated horse shook his bells in reply. The sleigh was a bright red affair with two seats. Suitcases were stacked on the floor; the three girls and an extra boy crowded in the back seat; and Tippy climbed up beside Theodosia and the driver, and pulled up their robe.

"If only you could telephone when you get there," Miss Tremaine mumbled through her scarf, braving the cold and standing on the steps, doing her duty by her pupils to the last. "Oh, dear, I hope you won't freeze."

"We're melting." Tippy's assurance was sincerely given, for she had on two sweaters and a fur evening jacket under her snow suit. She was mashed against Theodosia on one side and bound by the robe on the other until she felt like a papoose in a sling.

A shout went up from the windows as Annex collected himself for his take-off and the sleigh gave a lurch in the rut it had made. Bells jingled, arms waved, and little spatters of white confetti fell from an overhanging tree.

It was only a three-mile ride but it was a merry one. Annex trotted musically along. His sleigh was light on the frozen snow, the noise he made had a cheerful sound; and when he reached the West Point gate he received a fitting welcome.

One guard to wave him on would have been enough, but three came tumbling out to look at him. He grandly shook his bells for them before he slowed his clop-clop to a prancing, musical walk. Cadets, hurrying along on the sidewalk, bent their heads into the cold and walked backwards to watch his progress, and the Hotel Thayer's whole staff of bellboys came running out.

"Business must be bad," Theodosia commented, standing up and stretching. "Dot, you and Ellie will probably have the whole second class to yourselves. Meg and I can take the third, and Tippy, you can run the first. Shoot out the cases, girls."

She swung herself across Tippy who was still wound up in the robe, and down to the ground. Mr. Crane, who was fortunately thin, spread out a little and asked over his red muffler, "When you goin' to want me again?"

"As soon as you feed Annex," she answered carelessly. "Take him down to your friend's in Highland Falls and feed you both, then we'll ride up to Grant Hall." The horse was hot, his sides bellowed steamily, and she dragged the

robe from Tippy and swung it over him. "Good old Annex," she praised, and produced a lump of sugar.

It wasn't until they were upstairs in a room that Tippy
began to wonder how much this little adventure was cost-
ing Theodosia. Mr. Crane and his horse seemed to be engaged for the week end; and with Ellie and Meg next door
and the redheaded Dot gone off to find a roommate, she
thought she should ask and offer to share it.

"Pooh. Relax," was the only answer she got.

Theodosia whistled while she unpacked; and Tippy
hung away her borrowed clothing and felt excited over
giving West Point a shaking up. This was the time of year
cadets call the "gloom period": mid-seasonal weeks of
cold, snow, and rain, lasting through examination time
and until spring brings outdoor activities again and
promises a change. A horse hitched to a sleigh in a mech-
anized age, Tippy decided, should be a change.

She was the first one ready and outside again, and she
sang with the others as the sleigh jingled along the white,
crunchy avenue. Cadets would be easy to find today. The
junior guards need only call them from their warm rooms;
and she stamped into Grant Hall with the others, her stadium boots tracking snow, her red snow suit a bright
splotch of color.

Theodosia wore her coonskin cap like Daniel Boone
heading an expedition, and Tippy trotted along behind
in a fur-trimmed parka, like a happy Eskimo.

Peter, like all the others, was dressed for rough weather,
and he thought Tippy hadn't been so cute, so carefree and
sparkling for a long, long time. Since her return from

Washington, he had geared himself to a sweet, thoughtful
Tippy. The one who sat in front of him on a borrowed sled
and shrieked for speed was almost a stranger. She threw
a wicked snowball, too, with all her strength and deadly
aim. Bobby had met the first one.

The sleigh had toured a string of hastily borrowed sleds
to a steep hill behind the chapel. To lighten the load for
Annex, the boys gave helpful pushes on the upgrade and
the girls crunched along beside them. Only Bobby and
Theo rode like king and queen on the back seat of the
sleigh. They bowed and waved, and were being alto-
gether gracious to a bunch of plodding peasants when
Tippy let a snowball fly. It smacked Bobby in the face with
a stinging splatter and he was out from under the robe in
a flying leap. Peter watched her take to a steep bank and
send down a rain of missiles before Bobby caught her.
When she went down it was with both hands throwing
snow, and when she came up she was a sugar-coated cin-
namon drop and Bobby had more snow inside his wind-
breaker than clung to its waterproofed fabric.

Years of tussling with him had taught her self-protec-
tion. She knew how to drop her head and butt like a goat,
how to lock arms and kick the backs of his knees. When
he fell, she always managed to land on top and to roll out
from under when she was finally downed. She fought by
a system of skill and retreat; for when she could, she ran.
Her last escape got her back to the sleigh, and a dozen
hands boosted her up to safety.

"Oh, me," she gasped, clutching Mr. Crane for protection. "Bobby, don't you *dare* pull me out!" Then, "Eee-

eee-e. Stop him! Oh, help me! *Help me!*" She was going. Her legs were already out, and Mr. Crane was either going with her or be pulled in half.

Then Bobby sailed through the air. Peter lifted him by his shoulders, someone swung him by his feet, and he sailed off in a beautiful swan dive that both cooled and calmed him.

"Nice going, Tip," he said, coming up out of the drift and shaking himself. "I dare you to get out and try it again."

"No, thanks."

Tippy was safe and she intended to stay so. It took a lot of coaxing and the promise of a united front to put her on the sled again. And when a real snowball fight started, with an even number on each side and from behind the safety of a fort, she ducked whenever Bobby raised his arm.

He and Theodosia led the opposing team; and but for Peter's speed and deadly aim, they could have stormed across the narrow no man's land between. He sent pellets flying like machine-gun fire, and the others learned not to pack neat cannon balls, but to keep on firing.

The battle ended in a truce when Annex began to shake his bells and Mr. Crane called out, "Hey, you kids! I'm gettin' cold."

The game was over and the sides shook hands. Bobby's big black glove reached out to Tippy but she shook her head and backed away. "Oh, no you don't," she fooled him by saying. "I'd be the man on the flying trapeze." And she made Peter sit on the front of the sled going back, just in case there were a few snowballs hidden in the sleigh.

Once in the warmth of the Boodlers, she grinned at her wet hair and a scratch over one eye. "It was worth it," she said to Theo, slipping off her parka and trying to shake out the wet drops. I've never had more fun. Look at those two dopes out there."

Bobby and Peter were doing an apache dance. Bobby had his wet pants rolled up to show he was the girl, and Peter would throw him across the floor, bend him over a table, and go off and leave him. They always managed to meet again in a series of steps more like a cakewalk, and the Saturday afternoon idlers in the Boodlers cheered them on and begged for an encore.

"No can do," Peter panted, flopping into a chair and letting Bobby pick himself up from his last fling. "The guy weighs a ton. Who got me into this, anyway?"

"You got yourself, muscle-man Jordon," Tippy retorted. Another roughhouse had started in another part of the room, and she said reluctantly, "I'd better go and telephone my family where I am. Save my seat for me. I'll be back."

CHAPTER X

THE TELEPHONE gave its shrill authoritative summons. Colonel Parrish stopped pacing up and down the living room, up and down, and stood with his fists clenched.

"What shall I do, Marje?" he asked, afraid. "It might be Tippy. Shall I answer it?"

"No! Wait." Mrs. Parrish, too, seemed turned to stone. She sat, tense and still, in one corner of the love seat, and only her tear-filled eyes moved to look at him. "If it should be Tippy," she said slowly, "ask for Peter. Don't say anything—just talk to Peter. I know it seems cowardly, Dave, but it isn't. We aren't the ones to tell her. Ask for Peter."

The bell rang again, sharper and more insistent. The lines in Colonel Parrish's face grew deeper as he walked over to the little desk where it stood. His hand reached out, stopped, and left him staring down at a message written shakily on a scratch pad.

It had come an hour ago, first contact with the outside world on that still, Saturday afternoon; and it was from one of his oldest and closest friends, Colonel Prescott. *"Couldn't reach you by phone,"* his eyes saw now, and he ripped the page from the pad and crumpled it in his hand.

"Answer, Dave."

"I. . . ." He looked back in a silent appeal for help, then lifted the receiver. "Hello," he said in a voice so hoarse it sounded strange to him. "Colonel Parrish speaking."

"Dad?" a blythe voice flowed into the room, "this is Tippy. Remember me? I went off in a snowstorm and I'm having more *fun*. I just wanted to check and tell you I'm still alive. Did a letter come?"

"No—no letter."

"Well, I won't be home until after school on Monday. Hear the racket? I'm in the hall outside the Boodlers and we're having a wonderful time. If a letter comes you'll call me, won't you?"

"I. . . ."

"Dad, are you still there? Can you hear me?"

Tippy's voice sounded anxious and he made a brave effort to say, "I just turned around to find out what your mother was trying to ask me. She wants to talk to Peter if he's around."

"Oh, flirting, is she? Aren't you jealous?" Tippy broke off a laugh to call, "Peter? Oh, Peter Jordon. A beautiful *femme* calling for Peter Jordon." Then with a " 'By, Dad, see you on Monday," she left him waiting and wondering how he could frame the message he had to give.

It seemed a long time before Peter's deep voice rumbled into the telephone. Colonel Parrish pressed his hand against his forehead, trying to will order out of dizzy chaos; and when Peter said, "Sorry, Mrs. Parrish, to keep you waiting," he said in the same hoarse voice he had forced out for Tippy, "Son—Ken's gone. We can't break it to Tippy. Will you do it for us?"

"Sir . . . are you sure?" Peter, in the little booth where he had made so many nightly calls, sat down on the stool and asked again, "Oh, sir, *are* you?"

"Yes, Peter, I am. I had a telegram from his uncle who's

his nearest relative, and we've just talked to him. Ken died of wounds after he had been evacuated and placed in a hospital behind the lines. That's all he was able to learn."

"Sir. . . ." Peter could see Tippy far down the hall, talking to Bobby. She was saying something to him while he knotted her thick muffler and held her by its two plaid ends. Their faces were close together, laughing, teasing; then Bobby pulled her parka over her damp curls, gave the top of her head a pat, and shoved her away. "Perhaps Bob should be the one," he said. "I'll do it, sir, if you want me to, but Bob's here with us."

"Work it out anyway you can. I think she'll take it better from you. She trusts you." Colonel Parrish could say no more. He dropped the telephone back into its cradle and sat with his face in his hands. "Oh, Marje, Marje," he wept with tearless, wracking sobs. "That wonderful boy. And Tippy, our youngest."

"Don't, Dave. Oh, don't." Mrs. Parrish pushed her own heartbreak away and went to comfort him.

Peter sat alone in the booth. His mind was dazed and he couldn't think clearly. Ken Prescott . . . a guy he knew, a guy he liked . . . was gone. Ken was—dead.

Peter's hands were clammy as they gripped his knees and beads of cold perspiration broke out on his forehead. He had an order to carry out. But how? How could he tell Tippy? How would he tell her something he couldn't quite believe himself? How?

It seemed to be the only word he knew. Nothing else would fit with it, and he sat staring through the glass wall, numbly watching the group at the end of the hall. They were ready to leave. Tippy had pranced back into the

Boodlers and was out again with Theodosia. They made departing signals. They grinned farewell, and Peter's stiff face tried to grin in return. How was he to tell her?

He stood up to open the sliding door, then sat down and closed it again. His mind had begun to function now and it told him he needed a week end pass. Just why, he wasn't sure, but he knew he had to have it: and he dialed the Commandant's quarters.

"Peter?" Tippy called, and came sliding along the hall to say, "Really, if you and Mums are going to talk *forever*, you'd better let me in on it, too." She pushed open the door and asked, "What does she want?"

He had the pass. The Commandant was still talking so he had to listen. He was afraid Tippy might hear the rumble of a voice too deep to be her mother's, and he kept wondering how he was to express his appreciation in respectful terms. Finally he just said, "Thank you," and left off the "sir."

She stood there, waiting, leaning against the door with her eyes shining and her cheeks still pink from the snow Bobby had rubbed into them. "Oh, hurry up," she cried impatiently. "We have to walk all the way back to the hotel because Theo let the sleigh go home. The others have all gone but Theo and Bobby. Oh, Peter, hurry."

He wondered why she couldn't see his hand tremble when he zipped up his heavy football jacket and pulled on its hood. He pulled it on as far as he could to hide his face. Bobby and Theo had gone out and banged the thick door behind them.

"I never saw you so slow," Tippy laughed, and leaned out to peek around at him.

"I've lost my gloves," he mumbled.

"Right in my pocket."

There was nothing to do but let her pull him up and out; and as she bobbed along the corridor beside him, he had to listen to her say:

"We do have fun, don't we? Aren't you glad we're us?"

"You bet." How? How? How? There was no other word in his brain.

They had passed the junior guard at his desk; they were out in the cold, dark evening. Stars sparkled above the snow, icy whiteness crackled underfoot. Tippy's red arm was tucked through his and her woolly mitten waved as she talked of the still beauty around them. "Oh, Peter," she cried, "I love West Point!"

How? Other words began to fit with it. Simple words, like when, and where. How, and when, and where? Peter walked along, almost silent in her chatter, and was suddenly faced with the answer. He had to tell her now, before she hated her parents for letting her laugh and be happy when Ken was dead. Ken was dead. He had to tell her. He had to break her heart.

Peter looked up at the sky for help. Somehow, lifting his eyes to the vast star-studded heavens, brought him closer to God and the unseen help he needed. The lighted hotel was before them and was growing larger and larger. There was only the snowy street on one side of the deserted walk and a low stone wall on the other, so he stopped. "Tippy," he said, putting both arms around her, "you know I love you, don't you?"

"Yes, but Peter—not here." She tried to pull away and he had to hold her tighter.

"I love you," he repeated, "and I'd rather die than hurt you. But I have to, darling. Put your head against me because I have to tell you. Tippy, it's Ken."

He felt her sag. Her hands bit into his jacket sleeves, then she was quite still, with her face pressed against him.

"He's gone, Tippy," Peter said; and he looked up at the sky again. "Oh, God," he prayed silently, "help us. Help us, God."

There was no movement from Tippy. She was a statue in his arms. Her face was pressed against him; and when he pushed back her parka and stroked her cheek, he knew she didn't feel it. "Tippy," he said gently, "Tippy, darling."

She gave no answer. She took a deep, shuddering breath, then she was still again. They stood for a long time. Peter stroked her hair and tried to say words that might reach her. Then he bent down to pick her up and carry her the rest of the way.

"I can walk," she said, and took steady steps beside him.

Ken isn't in Korea, her mind kept telling her. He's at home. He'll be looking for me there. He'll come to me at home like he promised, so I must hurry. I must be there when he wants me. And her lips said silently, "I'm coming, Ken."

"Tippy, wait!"

Peter tried to hold her back but she pulled away. "I have to hurry," she said. "I know you don't understand, but . . . Ken's—*somewhere* . . . and I have to find him. I *have* to." And she began to run.

They were past the hotel when Peter stopped her and scooped her up in his arms. "We're going home," he told her. "Just as soon as your father comes. It will be quicker that way, darling."

"But I can't wait," she cried, struggling in his arms. "I have to be where he can find me. He knows about my room," she said with childish candor, "and the little chair and where my telephone is, so I have to be there."

"He's right here with you, Tip. Always. Ken knows where you are."

"He doesn't know I'm here because I shouldn't be here."

"You won't be, long." Peter felt her relax in his arms and dared set her gently down. He had so much to do. There was Bobby to find; perhaps a car to hire, should Colonel Parrish be unable to reach them; and he asked softly, "Could you come back to the hotel with me for a few minutes?"

"I don't care about my clothes. They're Theo's, anyway."

"Just till I can make some calls," he urged.

"No, I don't believe I could."

She said the words carefully, as if she really knew what they meant; and he was forced to point out, "But I can't leave you, Tippy."

"Why not?" The eyes she turned to him were big and dark as she stared at him. "I'm all right," she said. "It doesn't matter where you leave me. Nothing matters."

"Then walk back and wait outside."

He guided her around the arc of driveway and wondered what he should do when they reached the steps. If only she would cry. Tears, painful tears, would be far better for her than this numbed shock; and he stopped before the lighted doorway and said, "I have to hunt up

Bobby now. We need someone who can call your father."

"Don't worry about me."

She sat down on an icy step, and Peter doubted if she knew it was almost bitter cold now. A rising wind cut through his jacket and made him pull up the neck of his thick army sweater. Army sweater, he thought bitterly. Yea, for Army. Yea, for all the days Ken had spent learning to be a soldier. But he bent down to say, "I can't leave you here alone, Tip. Please come with me, darling."

Bright headlights turned into the driveway and picked them out: the small red bunch of Tippy, and Peter standing guard. Then a car stopped and Josh MacDonald sprang out.

"Gosh, I'm glad to see you," Peter said, going far enough away from her to say guardedly, "She's dazed, Josh. Shock, I guess. See what you can do."

"Tippy? Honey?" Josh knelt in the snow and put his arms around the still little figure. "I've come to take you home. We didn't think Dad should try to drive it in this weather and Penny's waiting for you at your house. Are you ready, honey?"

"Yes. I've been waiting to go." She stood up as Josh rose with her and said with her hand on his arm, "Perhaps we should tell Bobby, though. He might not want to go to a dance when Ken is—dead."

"I'll tell him."

Peter started up the steps but she reached out her other groping hand. "You'll come back, won't you?" she asked. "I hate to be so much trouble, Peter, but—will you please come back?"

"I'll be back. Don't go without me."

There was no sign of Bobby in the hotel lobby. The
dining room was almost empty and he tore down the stairway to the coffee shop. Bobby wasn't there either; and
that left no place for him and Theodosia to be, but at the
early movie. Peter scrawled a note at the desk and shoved
it at the clerk to slip in Theodosia's box beside her room
key, then ran out again and said, "It's all right, Tippy.
Bobby'll get the message when he brings Theo back. Come
on, let's get in the car."

"Are you going with us?"

"Yes, I'm going. Come on."

"I'm glad you are. I don't know why I should be glad,"
she said slowly, "about anything. But I'm glad you're
going. Ken would want you to. He'd be glad to know I'm
—looked after."

She let them put her in the middle of the wide seat.
Josh had to concentrate on the slippery driving, but Peter
watched her with anxious eyes. She sat with her mittens
clasped on her lap, her gaze on the white glare of snow in
the headlights' beam. Several times she drew in a shuddering breath; and when she sighed and said, "I'm such a
lot of trouble," they wondered what her thoughts were.

"Little sisters are never any trouble," Josh answered;
and Peter could only take her mittened hand in his and
hold it tightly.

CHAPTER XI

"TIPPY simply must cry," Penny groaned, late on Sunday afternoon, and with her own eyes red from weeping. "She doesn't cry, she doesn't eat, she doesn't sleep. She can't go on like this," she declared, throwing herself on the love seat.

"Tippy isn't like you," her mother answered wearily. "Did she take the sedative Dr. Martin left?"

"Yes, but it didn't work. It didn't put her to sleep."

"What is she doing now?"

"I don't know." Penny brushed her eyes and got up. "Yes, I do, too," she said. "She's just sitting in her room as she's been doing ever since she came home." She walked over to the piano and opened the little sewing basket Tippy had left there. It held a half-knitted olive-drab sock and a linen towel. "A.P.P.," she said, fingering the unfinished monogram. "Andrea Parrish Prescott. Poor little kid."

"Honey," Mrs. Parrish blinked back her own tears and asked, "can't you think of something we can try?"

"Not a thing. I hoped Switzy might break her down, but she only hugged him and looked up at me over his head and said, 'Ken won't ever see him again, will he? He knows what a comfort he is to me, though.' "

"Has Peter tried to talk to her this afternoon?"

"He made her go for a walk. We both thought the cold air might make her sleepy, but she came in and went straight upstairs again. She didn't argue about going and she talked about any subject he started: Ken, football, anything. She just—talked." Penny shrugged and closed the basket. "Do you think seeing the children would do the trick?" she turned around to ask.

"No, I don't believe so." Her mother shook her head. "Grief will come," she sighed, "and when it does, she'll suffer more than she is suffering now."

"But sometimes people—crack up," Penny reminded.

"Let's not think of that."

Mrs. Parrish went to the foot of the stairs to listen. Everything was still above, and she went on to the kitchen where Peter sat at the table with Trudy. He was drinking coffee, and she laid her hand on his shoulder and asked, "What time will you have to go back, Peter?"

"I ought to be in by seven but I can wait till eight. Alcie should be here by then, if Jon drives her up. She was clear down by Philadelphia, you know. Mrs. Parrish?" He brought her a chair and sat down again to face her. "What can I do for Tippy?" he asked. "I don't seem to help her but she keeps wanting me to stay. One minute she says, 'Oh, Peter, what would I ever do without you?' and the next she tells me that she's such a lot of trouble. She seems to think she's making it hard for everyone—for you and Colonel Parrish, for Penny, Josh, Bobby, me. I think she won't let herself go because she's afraid she'll worry us more. Can you see what I mean?"

"Yes. Yes, I do."

"At first," he went on, "it was shock. She didn't know what had hit her. Now she keeps trying to stay out of everyone's way. It's a sort of psychosis, or whatever you call it. Something has to snap her out of it."

"That's what Penny and I were saying."

"But what?"

Trudy had sat across the table without speaking. Now she pushed away her cup and stood up. "It's time to do something about that child," she said, "and I'm agoin' to do it."

Peter and Mrs. Parrish watched her march across the dining room and into the hall, and when she turned and went up the stairway, they followed stealthily behind her.

Tippy's door was open and she had changed into her white wool dress. "Hello, Trudy," she said into the mirror. "Is dinner ready?"

"No, child, it's only five o'clock." Trudy walked into the room and locked her hands together under her voluminous apron. "Tell me, honey," she asked softly, "why don't you let your heart out? You can cry in Trudy's arms, jus' as you always has. They's waitin' for you."

"There's nothing to cry about." Tippy switched off the dressing-table lamp and was hidden in the wintry dusk. "I'm just the same as I was yesterday," she said. "Ken was gone yesterday, only I didn't know it. I laughed and talked yesterday, so what's the difference today? He's been gone for a lot of days. I didn't even know it."

"But you knows it now. You *knows* it." Trudy uttered a silent prayer, "Oh, Lord, forgive me for hurtin' this child"; and she went on resolutely, "You knows Mr. Ken ain't ever comin' back to you. Not ever again. You can stay in this room for all the rest of your life, but you ain't ever goin' to see him walk in that door with his eyes shinin' an' his arms held out. You ain't ever goin' to have another little supper on that pretty cloth you showed me, with him passin' the napkins around and puttin' out the silver. You ain't ever goin' to dance together again, feelin' his arms around you an' havin' him hold you close to him an' smile down at you, like you say he always do."

"Trudy. Stop!"

Tippy buried her face in her hands, but Trudy talked cruelly on. She pushed deep into Tippy's numbed emotions and stirred them to a sluggish wakefulness by saying, "He ain't comin', Tippy. You're goin' to live all your days an' nights without him. There won't be no more letters to watch for, no weddin' in your long white dress an' Mr. Ken the proudest one there; an' there won't be no little house somewhere. You won't be bakin' cakes for him or be waitin' . . ." Trudy took a deep breath and said . . . "waitin' to hear him call you 'cherub.'"

A dry hard sob pushed through Tippy's hands. "Don't, Trudy," she whispered. "I'm trying so hard not to think of all that, and you hurt me so. There's Mums and Dad to remember and. . . . Oh, Trudy, I can't bear it! I cant' *bear* it!"

"There, there, baby. Come here, honey." Trudy's loving arms reached out and Tippy crumpled against her. "Cry, honey, cry," she crooned softly, rejoicing in the sobbing weight of grief she held. "My precious little child, my baby, my little girl we all loves so much."

Mrs. Parrish tiptoed to the doorway, but Trudy shook her head and went on stroking Tippy's hair and crooning. The healing tears came faster. Tippy's weight was almost more than she could hold but her soft voice never faltered. And when the sobs lessened to a tired, quiet flow, she asked, "Is you ready for Trudy to put you to bed now, honey?"

"No. Oh, *no!*"

"You ought to rest. You ain't rested for a long, long time."

"I can't. I want. . . . Oh, Ken."

"Maybe you could rest a little in the living room," Trudy suggested. "I reckon that's the best place."

Peter had stood helplessly in the hall. He had heard Trudy's voice and Tippy's sobs. He had wanted to steal quietly away but Mrs. Parrish clung so tightly to his arm he couldn't. There was nothing he could do except fill in as best he could for Bobby; and since she and Colonel Parrish seemed to feel he did, he supposed he was being of some use. At least it kept him standing there, and he pulled down his black sweater with its large gray A and stared miserably down at his shoes.

"Peter," Mrs. Parrish asked softly, "will you carry Tippy downstairs for us?"

"Why—sure."

She felt so light in his arms, such a feather of a girl. Her eyes were closed, her golden curls swept against his cheek; and as he laid her gently on the sofa, he dared touch them with his lips.

"Thank you, Peter," she murmured. "I hate to cause such a fuss." Then she turned her face into a pillow and began to cry again.

Trudy had started the tears and had left Peter to stop them. He took a rose afghan from Mrs. Parrish before she slipped away and laid it over Tippy. Then he sat down on the edge of the cushion and held her tenderly in his arms.

Tears of exhaustion rolled down her cheeks. They clung to her long dark lashes, then slipped in a silent stream down her cheeks and into the black knitted wool on Peter's chest. It grew dark outside. Night settled beyond the one lamp on the piano. Sometimes Colonel Parrish stood in the archway, or Penny, or Josh, but they stole silently away again and left him to his vigil.

"Peter?" Tippy's eyes opened when he had thought her safely asleep. "I'm hurting you," she said. "This terrible ache I have is what you feel for me, isn't it?"

"No, Tip."

"You mustn't." A trembling sigh shook her and she said again, "Don't love—anyone—too much."

"Go to sleep, darling." Peter's voice was gruff with emotion. "Your love for Ken is wonderful," he said. "You gave him everything he wanted, all your love. Just remember that, Tip. You're unhappy and suffering now because you did that for Ken. Every tear you shed is worth what you gave him."

"I hope so. Oh, Peter, I'm so tired."

"Then go to sleep."

Her amber eyes dropped then opened wide again. "You won't go away, will you?" she asked.

"Not till I have to."

"Poor Peter." She was still for a moment, safely quiet in his arms until she sighed and said, "I wish you'd go have your dinner with the others. It worries me. I know I'm such a bother."

"All right, Tip, if you want me to. I'd rather stay with you, but I'll go."

"I think I wish you would."

He slid himself off the cushion and put pillows under her head. "Go to sleep, little Tippy," he whispered, bending down to lay his cheek against hers. "We're all right here, and we love you."

The Parrishes were gathered around the kitchen table when he went out to them, sure Tippy was drifting into a restoring sleep; and Penny said, "We're eating out here because we didn't want Tip to hear us in the dining room. Did she go to sleep?"

"She will. She's pretty groggy."

Peter sat down and looked at the plate of food Trudy brought him. He had had no more sleep than Tippy, and very little to eat. Alone in Penny's guest room, he had put on a pair of Josh's pajamas and a robe, and had sat at the window, smoking an endless chain of cigarettes. Even in bed he had turned and tossed, until finally he had propped his pillows behind him, clasped his hands beneath his head, and lain staring into the dark until a first faint streak of light crept through the window. War had come a lot closer to West Point.

Peter wasn't afraid of war for what it could do to him. He told himself he would either fight through or black out, as Ken had. It was what it did to the other people. When you fought a war, you were busy. The ones who got the telegrams weren't. They just sat at home and waited for the blow to fall. Peter remembered Tippy's lifeless eyes and was bitterly glad they could never look so blank for him.

"I'm not hungry, thanks," he said.

"None of us are." Colonel Parrish pushed away his own plate of untouched food and took the cigarette Josh held out to him. "When you have to go back, son," he offered, "I'll drive you. I'd like to see young Bob for a minute."

"I should be leaving soon."

Peter thought of the promise he had made Tippy and stole in to look down at her. She was sound asleep but her breathing was ragged. She gave a quiet little moan while he watched her, jerked, and threw out her arms. He wanted to kiss her tear-stained cheek, to hold her again as he had been allowed to do for a precious hour, but he only turned away and went back to the hall.

"Alcie should be here soon," he said softly, grateful for the arm Colonel Parrish laid around his shoulders.

CHAPTER XII

So MANY DAYS crawled by. Alice had come to stay a week but Tippy refused to let her.

"Really, Alcie," she said in a tight, reasonable voice on Tuesday, "it wouldn't do any good. You're cutting classes and so am I. I think we should both go back to school tomorrow. Life has to go on, you know." They were in her room and she lifted the lid of the big chest at the foot of her bed. "Once I needed a decent education for Ken, but now I need it just for something to do. Here, I want you to have this tablecloth."

"Oh, Tippy, I can't take it."

"I want you to. I'll keep the other stuff I bought or made, but I can't look at this." She walked over to the window and said with her shoulders square, "Perhaps I'm going to be like Theo, and push all sentiment out of my life."

Alice looked down at the box on her lap and shook her head. "I don't think you will be," she said thoughtfully. "Perhaps, for a while, you'll have to have some sort of protective crust, but not always."

"It isn't as if I'd been *married* to Ken," Tippy told the white snow outside. "That way, I could have a decent grief. I could shut myself up and be alone. I wouldn't have to go to college and pretend things are just the same. Death is supposed to hurt *married* people, but not girls."

"But it does, Tip," Alice answered, knowing how much

153

it would hurt her. "If I lost Jon today, it would be just as hard as ten years from now. Being married doesn't matter."

"That's what I'm trying to say. My grief is just as hard to bear, but I'm not supposed to let Mums, and Dad, and Penny, and Josh, and Trudy, and Peter, and Theo, and all the girls at school see how I feel. It isn't considered *suitable* for a girl to grieve openly. Oh, she can cry and fly off and lose her temper so that people will say, 'Poor thing, she's nothing but a bundle of nerves,' but just to look sad or to sit and remember? It isn't done. It upsets too many other people. You see, there isn't any estate to settle or furniture to dispose of, or any decision to make about whether you'll stay where you are or come home. You are home. There's nothing to talk about or any reason to keep bringing it up. Nothing's any different in your life, except —you've had a telegram."

"I see what you mean."

"I wish I could go away somewhere."

"Where, Tip?"

"To visit Ken's people. But he doesn't have any. I wish he had a mother so we could talk about him, about when he was a little boy. I'd like to stay in the room he had and look at all the junk he collected. Bobby has a lot of junk, boxes of it. And some girl could sit with Mums, and they could talk about him and cry together."

She had lost her fine self-control and she turned back from the window. "I'm sorry, Alcie," was all she had time to say before she threw herself face down on the bed and burst into irrepressible sobs.

There were times in every day like that. Times when

nothing could hold back the ache in her chest. Usually she drove her car to the side of the road and let despair engulf her there, let her tears bathe her heartache, so that she could dry her eyes and go back to her family like a smiling, white ghost.

A week went by, two weeks of calm enduring, then Ken's last letter came.

Colonel Parrish took it from the mailbox, for Tippy never walked down the driveway now. He stood with it in his hand, studied the War Department envelope, the carefully typed address, then carried it back to the house.

"I don't know what to do with it, Marje," he said to his wife, in their little sitting room. "I have a feeling it's the last letter the boy ever wrote. How shall I give it to her?"

"Put it on her dressing table," she advised, looking at her watch. "It's almost time for her to come from school. Poor child."

He still stood, holding the white envelope, and she shook her head. "You can't stand by while she reads it, Dave. She'll want to be alone."

"I suppose so, but—oh, Marje, isn't there *something* we can do?"

"Nothing, Dave, nothing." And he went off with the letter, to leave it where Tippy would see it when she came home.

It was a white blotch in the February gray, for the snow had melted and settled into dingy piles and the sky was stormily preparing to send down more. Colonel Parrish started to leave the room then went back and turned on all Tippy's lamps. He picked up the letter again and laid it on the table beside her favorite chair. It seemed so little to do for her, he thought with a sigh, as he went down-stairs to watch for her.

She drove in slowly. She was always reluctant to come home and just as reluctant to leave again. There was no place where she wanted to be. She stopped her car, slipped out and stood looking at the dreary world around her. It could be such a beautiful world, she thought. The sad orchard could be only comfortably asleep, the little brook could be adventuring instead of dismally fighting the ice for its freedom, if only—Ken were coming home. She took her books from the car, closed the door carefully, and walked past the bay window where Switzy always waited for her.

Switzy's yelps of joy were her one real welcome. No matter how many others were there to meet her, to take her coat and kiss her in silent sympathy, she always stooped to hold his wriggling body. "Hi, Dad," she said, seeing her father and stopping Switzy's endless leaps by putting her books on a chair and sliding out of her coat. "Down, Switzy. I'll play with you in a minute. We had a stupid lecture, Dad. Where's Mums?"

"Upstairs." Colonel Parrish walked up the stairway be-side her, his arm around her shoulders, and at the top he gave her a loving squeeze. "Go to your room first," he said, "and—well, fix your hair." Then he turned back along the railing to the sitting room.

Tippy went on through the hall. She saw the letter when she reached her door and stopped to stare at it. Her hand reached out to close the door but Switzy whined and she had to let him in. He took so long. He brought his ball and jumped against her, pleading for a game, and she had to sit down in her little chair and hold him on her lap. He drew back his lips and grinned at her with the cute trick Ken had taught him, and his teeth snapped at her collar until she had to hold him down with her elbows. "Don't, Switzy," she said absently, trying to tear open the outer envelope with shaking fingers. It was only a formal thing and she let him have it and take it under the bed. Then she sat staring at the second, precious one.

It had Ken's handwriting on it. It was all she had of him now, the paper he had touched. Slowly, carefully, she worked at the flap, trying not to tear it. And she breathed a little sigh of relief when it came loose. There were his words, his last message to her. She crouched lower in her chair and began to read.

My cherub:

I can only say I hope you will never read this letter. But if you should, I want you to know you were my last conscious thought. Don't grieve, my precious one. Love me always, as I'll love you wherever I am. Keep me deep in your heart; but let the love we've had lead you on to another love that will fulfill the good life we planned.

I'm trying to tell you this, Tippy, because you must go on. If you have this letter, I know you're crying. Don't, my darling, don't cry. I love you so much that your grief will hurt me more than leaving you. Be happy, cherub. Not now, I know you can't right now, but someday. You have such a great gift for giving happiness, and I want you to be happy, too. Remember that. And remember, too, that it's up to you to build a life for both of us. I love you so.

Tippy held the letter against her and stared above it at the wall. "Oh, Ken," she whispered, "my wonderful darling, you don't know what you're asking. I can't build a life. I can't—I can't. I don't want anyone but you. Can you hear me, Ken?"

She waited a long time, straining to hear an answer, then laid her head on the table and began to sob.

Switzy crawled out from under the bed and pawed at her knee. He pushed his fuzzy little face under her crossed arms and licked the tears from her cheeks. He climbed back onto her lap and whined for notice, then he gave a worried little grunt and settled down against her.

It was dinnertime. Tippy pulled up her head and sat for long minutes with her forehead in her hand. She must go on. Ken had known it and had tried to help her. She must go downstairs where the television set was showing a cowboy film. She must smile at her mother and father across the candles on the dinner table and must remember to praise Trudy's apple dumplings. She could do all that. She could live an ordinary life, day by day by day. But plan for a future with someone else? She shook her head. "No, Ken," she said with the letter against her cheek. "There can't ever be anyone else."

Switzy stirred and she carried him over to his basket. He gave a contented wag because she was doing familiar things again, and kept his black, beady eyes on her when she laid Ken's letter under her pillow and came back to brush her hair. She stood before the mirror for a long, long time; just stood, as if she weren't quite sure what a brush was for or what she was seeing in the glass, so he got up and trotted over. He touched her lightly with his paw, a gentlemanly, reminding pat, and she turned and looked down at him. "Thanks, Switz," she said. "I'll hurry."

And so the days went by. Spring made several attempts to waken, and finally accomplished it in a burst of yellow and green. The sun added rose and blue and red to the color scheme and set the stage for June week at West Point and Alice Jordon's wedding.

Tippy accepted the wedding and let herself be fitted for her maid of honor's dress, but she said to her mother, "I can't go to all those graduation things with Peter, Mums; I can't."

"He's counting on it, honey," her mother replied sadly. "He's been down here whenever he could manage a week end and it seems a shame to let him down."

"I know it does." Tippy tried not to remember how faithful Peter had been or how much she had depended on him during these last few months; on his nightly calls, his selfless thought of her. "I know I ought to go," she sighed, "but I don't want to."

"And of course there's Bobby," her mother reminded. "He wants to show you off and have us all there when he marches in the last review. And Peter should have a girl for the Superintendent's reception."

"He could borrow Theo, or perhaps Alcie would go." Tippy got up to walk aimlessly about the living room. "I don't see why he hasn't found himself a girl," she said unhappily. "Even Maxsie Green, who's pining for him. I wish he would."

"He never will." Mrs. Parrish shook her head and said with positive directness, "He won't, Tippy, and you may just as well make up your mind to it. He loves you as much as you love Ken, and I'm afraid the boy will never change."

"Has he ever said so?" Tippy stopped beside the piano and looked back at her mother. "Has he, Mums?" she asked again.

"Once. He told your father and me. He said he wanted us to know it, since he's here so much."

Mrs. Parrish thought about the day, a few weeks before, when Peter had stood on their flagstoned terrace. He had held his cadet cap in his hands and his gray eyes had looked directly at Colonel Parrish when he said, "I suppose you know I love her. It sounds easy to say you'd die for a person, but I would. I'd change places with Ken if I could. That's how deep it goes. I want Tippy to be happy even more than you do."

Mrs. Parrish knew it was no use to tell Tippy that. It would only make her more hesitant to turn to him for comfort and companionship, so she said, "We've always known it, though."

"Oh, dear." Tippy walked on to the window. "I still don't want to go," she said. "I want to see him graduate, but I don't want to see him in his uniform afterward. I can't bear the sight of young officers in uniform, and I'm only going to be in Alcie's wedding because it's a civilian affair. I *hate* West Point!"

"Then, honey, can't you think of Peter?"

"I'm trying to. I'm trying to think of everyone in the world but myself. Oh, Mums," she cried in distress, "can't you see how hard it is to keep pushing myself to do the things I should? Ken wants me to. If it weren't for that, I wouldn't even try. But there are just some things I feel as if I can't bear to do—and June Week's one of them."

"Then I wouldn't worry, dear. Peter will understand because he always does, and Bobby won't mind."

"Bobby." Tippy looked despairingly at her mother. "He's been so darned sweet," she groaned. "Not like Bobby at all, but just really sweet, and kind of pathetic in his effort. He hunts up ridiculous post cards and mails them to me, and he sent me those pitiful flowers. They looked as if they'd been left over from the week before, but he sent them. And he hasn't been grouchy or fussy, not once. I'll think up something I can do for him. Here comes Penny." She opened one of the French windows and went out to stand on the terrace.

"Hi," Penny called, slamming the door of her station wagon. "I've come to take you into town with me."

Someone was always coming to take Tippy somewhere. Colonel and Mrs. Parrish had suddenly become too helpless to drive themselves, and Penny or Alice were always running in to carry her off.

"We're coming out again right after the play and bringing a sort of nice man with us," Penny explained as she came over to the terrace and picked a rose on her way. "I thought you might spend the night and help me entertain him. Here." She stuck the pink blossom in Tippy's curls, and said, "That's very becoming, cherub," and caught her breath in shocked dismay.

"It's all right." Tippy tried to smile but a sudden pain shot through her chest and tears filled her eyes. "I've just been feeling sort of mopey," she said quickly, "because

Mums has been saying I should go up to Peter's graduation. I don't want to go."

"You should though. Life's full of things we don't want to do, pet," Penny answered, slipping her arm around Tippy's waist. "I don't want to leave my children every night and say a lot of stupid lines from eight-forty to ten-forty-five, but I have to."

"I might say them for you," Tippy offered, glad for the light conversation that always seemed to flow where Penny was. "Goodness knows, I know them all."

"I'll bet you could. Now if I were to say," Penny dropped her voice to a near bass and rumbled, " 'Really, my dear, you're making too great an issue over a child. . . .' "

"Then I'd answer, 'But he's *my* child, Norman.' "

"Bravo!" Tippy had given a good imitation of Penny and she applauded it. "Would you like to do some radio work, or television, pet?" she asked. "I could help you get a job."

"If I do, I'll let you know. Just now, no thanks. I couldn't, Penny," she said seriously. "I have a couple of more weeks at Briarcliff, and I've decided I *will* go up to June Week and I *will* show more interest in Alcie's wedding. I know I'm being terribly difficult and ungrateful."

"Oh, but you aren't, pet." Penny shook her head in vehement denial. "I'd cry such an ocean of tears the family would be forever sloshing around in them," she said. "I'd never have been able to go back to that darned school."

"The teachers all send you their love every now and then," Tippy remembered to pass on.

"Why? I nearly drove them crazy when they had me. Such emoting! Such desperation because I had to have an education before I could commence to begin to become an *actress*. Well," she said flatly, "I began. I am."

"And you'll keep the offer open for me?" Tippy asked.

"You know I will. I'll help you every way I can."

Tippy thought a great deal about Penny's suggestion during the following weeks. It fluttered before her like a banner of hope. Her sewing basket was packed away in the locked chest and she made no more cakes and pies in the kitchen. Marriage with Ken had been the only career she had wanted. She knew she was different from Penny, that she would never be a success or even a persistent actress, but she had so many hours and weeks and years to fill. And one day, on impulse, she drove up to talk to Bobby about it.

He always came out to the car with such solemn tenderness that it would have been amusing had it not been so sweet. And he always gave her a pawing pat before he crawled in and sat beside her. Today, he listened with his head cocked like Switzy when she was about to throw his ball, and he said too glibly when she finished, "I'll bet you'd be a wow. Television stations would simply *snap* you up! Like that."

His fingers popped like a firecracker under her nose, and made her laugh. She laughed with such spontaneous enjoyment that Bobby grinned with her and wondered what else he could do to be a comic; and he said, "You know, I've been thinking about taking a job this summer. I have two whole months to loaf away, and not much cash, so I've considered soda-jerking in the village. I could eat all the free boodle I want, too; but maybe I won't." He stretched his long legs out and decided complacently, "We might both get jobs in New York."

Tippy wondered what paying concern would want him, but she let him dream on and say, "We could travel back and forth together in your car and I'd be on hand to take you to lunch and see that you ate."

"What if some other girl should want to take you, free, gratis, and for nothing?" she couldn't resist asking. "You'd meet dozens of rich girls."

"I'd tell 'em nothing doing. Not even if they suggested the Colony or the Stork."

"You'd turn down *those* for an Automat?"

"Well," he wrinkled his brow and gave her a dubious grin. "No," he admitted, "but I'd take you along."

Bobby was a lamb. Both he and Tippy were stars in a television studio and he was the backbone of the whole organization before he decided he had pumped enough nonsense into her for one day and it was time to turn to his own affairs. "Come up any time," he invited largely. "But kindly bring a cake. I have to go now."

Something bright went with him. Tippy sat in the car and watched him hustle through the archway that led to his stern, monastic barracks. His heart would never break. Alcie hadn't scarred it; Theo couldn't. War? Tippy sat and shook her head.

How could four children, she wondered, all in one family, have so many different kinds of hearts? David's beat with a steady rhythm; Penny's changed like a record player that gives forth any kind of song; Bobby's was a tough, durable affair. And hers? She gripped the wheel and sighed. "Mine's the kind that breaks from one blow and doesn't heal properly," she said. "It isn't a very strong, reliable heart."

CHAPTER XIII

"I DID IT," Tippy told Ken's picture. "Somehow I went through it, and no one but you and I knows how hard it was."

June Week was over. Summer dresses littered her bed and a floppy leghorn hat, wreathed in roses, trailed its black velvet ribbons over the chest. Tippy had worn the hat and a pink organdy dress at the Superintendent's garden party. She had gone down the receiving line with Peter and had stood beside him, sipping punch and eating little cakes. It was the graduating class's most important social event, for the cadets would be officers tomorrow and were guests of honor today.

Discipline was over. The Superintendent gripped their hands heartily and smiled at the pretty girls they presented. He knew some would be married tomorrow. The chapel was already massed with white flowers and candles, ready for the weddings that would keep the chaplains busy all day.

"I know this child," he took Tippy's hand and said. And he looked inquiringly at Peter. "Haven't I heard that you two. . . ." he began, before a furtive jab from his wife's elbow stopped him. He remembered then what his good friend Dave Parrish had told him about the death of one of his favorite boys, and was relieved to hear Peter say quickly:

"It's my roommate, sir. He's being married."

"Ah, yes. Young McKettrick. I knew there was some connection. It's nice to have you here, Tippy."

"Thank you, General." Tippy had been passed along the line.

"The remark didn't hurt as much as poor Peter thought it did," she whispered to Ken's picture. "For some reason I felt as if he were saying it about us. I'd been pretending I was with you and I felt—I felt almost pleased." She sighed and said carefully, "Most of the time I didn't do that, darling, pretend we were together. It was Peter's graduation and I tried to enjoy it with him. He didn't know, Ken, how lonesome I was."

Peter had known. He had looked forward to this graduation day for four long years. He had planned it. When he had been a plebe, he had told his roommate, much in the vernacular of Bobby, "Boy, when I get out of here I'll show them something."

"What?" Gilbert McKettrick had asked, with his future safely settled. Gilbert would marry the girl next door and become a sober officer; but he watched Peter grind himself down on his hard desk chair and expound fiercely, "I'll throw this darned uniform so far it never will land. I'll be *tough!*" And when he was a third classman, overlord of the plebes, he grinned and decided, "When I graduate, if I ever do, I'll hate to leave this joint." And at the end of his summer's leave and returning as a second classman, he had displayed Tippy's photograph more openly and declared, "Here's the girl you're going to see around from now on. Come graduation day? Oh, man!"

Now it *was* graduation day, and Tippy was farther from him than she had been when he hung her picture on his locker door. She danced and smiled and ran around the post with the other girls; she swung hands coming down the steep hill from chapel; she clapped pridefully when the corps marched. He knew she would even kiss him when he came out of the Field House with his diploma. But so would Alcie; so would Jenifer, just home from England; so would Gwenn, in her movie-struck way. Tippy would be the quiet one. She would wait for a peeress, a glamour gal, and next-week's bride to have first chance.

"I was awfully proud of him, Ken," Tippy said, setting the photograph down and sitting with her arms crossed to smile at it. "I couldn't help but be. When he walked up for his diploma, he got more cheers and applause from the corps than anyone else in the whole graduating class. He had to stand and wait until it stopped. And he looked so sweet. Somehow, I thought about him getting ready— just brushing and brushing his hair till it lay flat, and fumbling to get his cuffs straight, and making his brass buttons go through the holes, the same way I do when I'm excited and nervous; and then, trying to walk downstairs and get in formation as if it really weren't anything at all. And I thought that perhaps he'd taken down the picture of me when he slammed his locker door for the last time —and it hurt, Ken. It hurt to think of him looking around his room where he won't ever live again, and not being as happy as Gil McKettrick. I loved him. I loved him such a lot, and I felt sorry and sad. I wanted to do something for him that would make him know how I felt, but I didn't know what to do."

Tippy lifted her head and saw again the special little crowd that had waited for Peter after the exercises were over. General Jordon commanded it; gruff, genial, and with his girls around him, his younger children bunched a little to one side, like a chorus. They took up a good share of the crowded space; and when Peter came out, they all swooped forward. Tippy stood with her mother and father, and watched them surround him.

There was the fairy Bitsy, prancing up and down and talking like a Britisher through a missing front tooth; the tall boy who had been such a pale little nephew before he went to live in England; the twins, and Vance, clean for once in his life; and the sweet, quiet daughter, with her husband who would someday be the Earl of Esterbrook. Of course there was Alcie, too, Tippy reflected. And Gwenn—important and rather silly Gwenn, overdressed and glad to be away from the husband she had left in Hollywood. Tippy put her head down on her arms and sighed. "Oh, Ken," she whispered, "why couldn't you have come from a big family like that? I wouldn't be so lonely now."

They were all so proud. General Jordon boomed and pumped until Peter's arm almost came unhinged and the others had to crowd him away. Peter hugged them all and met the dark-eyed Cyril's handclasp with a brotherly fondness; but through it all, Tippy saw his eyes searching for her. Each time, they looked above a head and swept the crowd.

"I knew he was waiting for me, Ken," she said, remembering, "but I didn't want him to. I didn't want things to be the way they were. I don't know how to explain it, but I wanted him to have *everything:* his family and a girl to love him. Something inside me kept saying, 'It doesn't matter about you any longer, Tippy, so make him happy.' I wanted to, but I couldn't. I just stood there and clung to Mums, while I wished I could walk up and put my arms around him and kiss him the way his eyes begged me to. I couldn't, Ken. And when he left his family and came over to us, I gave him a sort of feeble peck that didn't mean a thing. I think he wished I hadn't done it at all."

Tippy sighed again and remembered the way she and Peter had walked across the Plain. They were just any couple among the hundreds that drifted toward the quadrangle to watch another class of plebes become third classmen.

"I'll have to get into uniform now," he said, "if I'm to be best man for Gil in an hour. Will you stay for the wedding?"

"Not if I'm to drive to Governors Island with you," she answered. And she tried to explain, "My clothes are in such a mess, and I'll have to press and repack them if I'm to be at your house for a week. Could you drive over and pick me up?"

"Sure."

To repack her clothes had been important. By doing it, she could miss a military wedding. Yet here they lay, tumbled about the room. "Ken," Tippy leaned forward to plead, "what am I going to do about this whole week at Peter's, and Alcie's wedding? What will I do about the whole month of leave he has? What will I do about all the rest of my life, Ken? Can't you help me?"

She gripped the leather frame with both hands and clung to it. "Help me, darling," she whispered frantically. "I'm so alone and—frightened."

A noise in the hall cut off her words. Trudy was coming for the dresses to be pressed, and Tippy pushed back on the dressing table bench. "Come in," she looked up to say, suddenly busy with a fingernail. "I don't need all this stuff, do you think?"

"Child, I wouldn't know." Trudy looked at the cottons, the afternoon and evening gowns, flung carelessly about, and remarked dryly, "I can't see how you managed to wear them all."

"I wore some of them twice," Tippy answered. "And I wore a bathing suit that's still in the car. June Week," she pointed out, trying to sound light, "is very dressy when you drag a first classman. Who's that coming up?"

"Miss Penny."

"What's she doing here?"

"She's on her way to town for a matinee and she brang Parri for us to keep. Joshu has a cold."

Tippy sprang up and met Penny at the door. "Do you want me to go over and stay with Joshu?" she asked. "I know how frightened you always are."

"Of course not, silly." Penny laughed and cupped Tippy's chin in the palm of her hand, while she scolded, "You've been doing too much baby sitting lately. You're no spinster aunt who glides in and out of peoples' lives whenever she's needed. Is she, Trudy?"

"I been tellin' her that."

"You're *young*, pet. I know you don't think so." She sat down on the edge of the bed to ask, "But isn't it already a little—easier?"

"Sometimes," Tippy admitted.

"It has to be. Our systems couldn't take it if it weren't. Pain *has* to lessen, Tip. Anything I can do for you?"

"No, thanks."

"Then I'll run along. Tell Mums, if she comes home before you leave, that I'll pick up Parri in the morning. And by the way," she turned in the door to say carelessly, "if any of the out-of-town wedding guests want to see my play, I'll manage some tickets for them."

Penny was always thoughtful, and Tippy ran to hug her. Tickets for *One Step to Heaven* were being sold in advance for next October; and she cried, "Oh, thank you, Pen."

"Pooh. Remember what Mums used to tell us?" Penny asked.

"What?"

" 'Smile up your face.' She used to say it whenever we looked glum or unhappy, and sometimes I wanted to murder her for it. Funny, but it always helps. Give Alcie my love and tell her I'll be there for part of the reception if I can make it."

She went off down the hall and Tippy turned back to open a drawer and take fresh lingerie from it. She glanced at Trudy who was busy at the bed, parted two slips and slid Ken's picture between them; then she laid the pile in the bottom of her empty case.

"Miss Penny turned out to be about the most sensiblest child I has," Trudy pronounced, straightening up with an armload for her pressing board. "Seems kind of unexpected. You goin' to take those beat-up shoes?"

"My loafers? I don't think so. I won't be walking much

except through the stores. And *now* who's banging around outside?"

Trudy, already in the hall, called back, "It's only Mr. Peter. He has a bundle and is goin' into your papa's sittin' room, and he says not to bother to come, for you'd better kind of hurry. He looks mighty handsome."

Tippy repacked all the things she needed. There was no Ken to talk to now. It was Peter who was waiting. Lieutenant Peter Jordon. Not Peter in cadet clothes, the boy whom she had known for a long time and was accustomed to seeing, but Peter in the same uniform Ken had worn. Peter, exactly the same, to shirt, tie, regulation blouse. And she thought desperately, I can't bear to see him. I don't *want* to go with him."

"Tip?" his voice called from the hall, and made her stop and close her eyes. "Mind if I come in?"

She had to look at him sometime, so she shook her head and forgot he couldn't see her answer. "Oh. Why, yes, come in," she remembered, and stood up straight to face him.

But the same old Peter lounged in the door. He wore a pair of gray slacks she had seen many times, and a white shirt with a bright, striped tie. "Just thought I'd be comfortable," he explained.

"You did it for me." Tippy took a few steps and clasped grateful arms around his neck. "Oh, Peter," she said, looking up at him, "you did it because you knew I'd feel exactly as I did. You shouldn't have, though."

"I took my first salute at the gate," he answered. "That was enough. And if putting on a pair of old pants can

make you look at me the way you're doing, I'll go around
in an Indian blanket if you want me to."

"I don't. But you shouldn't have done this. You spoil
me, Peter," she said. "I didn't tell you properly this morning how proud I am of you. I didn't do it right, at all."

"You did the best you could, Tip."

"No, I didn't. I am proud." She looked soberly into his
eyes then slid her hands down along his narrow face. "I'm
very proud," she said, when they met and held his chin.
"Will you believe me?"

"Always, Tip."

"Will you put your uniform back on?"

"Not today. I'd rather go back to being the kids we used
to be. I'd rather, Tip. Things hurt me, too."

"Then let's have fun. Let's be the old Peter and Tippy,
and run Alcie's wedding, shall we?"

"Straight into the ground." He gave her a hug, picked
up her big hat and clapped it on her head. "What gives
with all this junk?" he asked, while she ran about slamming things into her case.

"How you goin' to carry these?" Trudy asked, when
they clattered down the stairs. "You ain't goin' without
your dresses, is you?"

"We'll lay them on the back seat of Peter's fine new
graduation present," Tippy answered; and she added
sternly, "No, Switzy, you can't go. Parri, you can't, either."

Two disappointed faces synchronized their wails.
Switzy dropped his head and whined, but Parri threw
back hers and howled. She didn't really care if Tippy went
away. Her own parents were always leaving her and she

never made a fuss. It was simply fun to make more noise than Switzy; and her shrieks changed to giggles of delight when Peter tossed her up in the air and caught her. But Switzy was not so easy to comfort. He drooped and looked like the horse in *The End of the Trail.*

"We might take him," Peter suggested. "Our Rollo likes other dogs. They could pal around together."

"At a wedding? Don't be silly." Switzy was something better left at home. He was a link with Ken. "Look here, Switzy," she said severely, "you aren't going." And she took the dresses from Trudy and piled them in Peter's arms. "Scoot out with these," she ordered, just as she once would have done, "and be careful of them or I'll make you press them again. I'll be there in a minute."

Her case was still where he had set it, and she felt around inside it for the photograph of Ken. "I can't take you either, darling," she told it, running back up the stairs. "This is Peter's time. June Week was, too, but I muffed it. He took off his beautiful new uniform for me and this is the least I can do for him."

She set the likeness on her dressing table, whispered, "I love you, Ken," and ran back down again. "I'm ready," she called, giving Trudy and Parri kisses and Switzy a forgiving pat. "Such a commotion. You'd think I'm going off to stay a year."

Peter's uniform was neatly hidden under her pile of dresses and she pulled it out by its hanger and hung it on a little hook above the window. "Mighty careless, Lieutenant," she said lightly, shifting the shoulders to hang straight and even smoothing the sleeves. Then she climbed into the club coupé that was painted a dark, rich green because she had once said green was her favorite color for cars.

Peter slid under the wheel and pushed and pulled buttons in an exploratory way. "Darned if I can remember what all the gadgets are for," he remarked uneasily. "I got down here all right but my foot went around and around like a windmill, hunting for a clutch which isn't. Oops."

Liquid sprayed the windshield. It shot up like a geyser, and he muttered, "Thought I was turning on the air control. What the heck runs the wipers?"

Tippy worked buttons with him. The water stopped because its container had run dry, but when the motor roared, a blast of heat came with it. Their two heads were close together while they twisted fine chromium knobs that had no identifying letters on them. Wipers squeaked back and forth, headlights flared, and a small flashing light informed anyone behind them that they were turning left. And at last Tippy opened the glove compartment and took out an instruction book the company had thoughtfully provided.

"It's been so long since I've driven a car," Peter said, "and that old rumblebunny of Dad's has a gear shift. Read that again."

Tippy found a paragraph marked "Heat control," and they stopped the hot air pouring out. Nothing they could find would start the cold, even though they turned themselves upside down to feel under the dash for vents. Peter got out to close the hood that had popped up from one unlucky pull on a knob; and Trudy called from the steps, "Ain't you goin'?"

"We hope so."

They decided that their feet weren't hot. A draft from both above and below, they told each other, would be too much on such a cool day; so Peter mopped the perspiration from his forehead and Tippy slipped off the jacket to her linen dress.

The car slid off like a dream. It was a good car, and it told them so by silently tending to business. Peter was proud of it. He was like every man with his first new car; and his pleasure reminded Tippy of Ken, in Germany, with his. Ken had made a prideful, sweeping gesture and said, "The works. It's pretty, isn't it?"

You mustn't think of Ken, she reminded herself sternly. Ken's car belonged to a German family now. And she moved closer to Peter and said gayly, "I like the way you drive. You're about the best driver in the whole world—I betcha."

CHAPTER XIV

"ALCIE, you'll simply have to hold still," Tippy cried despairingly.

She sat on the floor in a thin cotton negligee and Alice stood above her in her wedding gown. Layers of white lace and net spread in soft folds over a satin hoop, and Tippy was trying to smooth out a few stubborn places that refused to flow gracefully into a long, spreading train. "Turn a little."

"I'm so nervous," Alice wailed, not daring to cry but wishing she could from sheer exhaustion. "All the parties we've had, and all the last minute shopping! If Gwenn hadn't insisted on giving that bust at the Waldorf last night. . . ." She leaned over and asked anxiously, "Have you seen Jon around?"

"Natch. He's chipper and cheerful. He's just as big today as he ever was, and looks like a Viking who's wandered in by mistake. There you are."

She slid back on her hands to gaze at the bride above her. Alice's hair hung softly straight as it always did, under a little Dutch cap of lace and seed pearls. Her brown bangs were a dark roof above her big gray eyes, and her cheeks were flushed from nervous excitement.

"You're about the cutest-looking bride I ever saw," Tippy told her. "You don't look old enough to be married. You look like one of those cute little dolls you see in showcases."

"I feel more like a bassinet with lace curtains," Alice answered. "What time is it?"

"Twenty-two minutes past seven. Now stand still while I slide into my own dress." A knock sounded on the door, and she called, "If you're Jonathan, you can't come in."

"I'm Peter."

"Oh. Well, wait a minute." She scrambled up and went over to open the door a crack.

"There's been a hitch," he whispered, and she slipped outside. "Dad wants me to wear my uniform," he told her. "Do you mind?"

"Why, of course not! There'll be hundreds of uniforms at the wedding, if the whole post comes. I'm on an army post."

She had left her sensibilities at home with Ken's picture. She had left her real self, too, and had brought along the Tippy who used to live on Governors Island. The one who swung frantically at a tennis ball, danced to a record player, shopped tirelessly, and breezed through the Jordon house like a member of the family, always ready to come, go, and stay up all night. "Wear it, Peter," she said. "I'd like to see you in it."

"First he wanted o.d., and now he's changed to blues. I hadn't planned to wear them," he said, worried and ruffling up his hair, so freshly combed, "but the old guy's all done up in his special evening dress, so I think I should. He's charging around in there like a nervous rooster. His white tie's crooked and his tails are flapping like wash on the line. How are *you* coming?"

"My bride stayed calm till a minute ago. I'd better go back."

Tippy slid through the door again and grinned at Alice who hadn't moved. "Your pa's gone berserk," she said pleasantly. "He's forgotten how well he did at Jenifer's wedding."

"Poor dear," Alice answered. "I'm glad he'll have Jen to sit with. I have to go to the dresser. May I walk?"

"If you stay on the sheet."

Alice let Tippy carry her train so she could find a lipstick and a piece of cleansing tissue. "I did so want Jenifer for my matron of honor," she said, holding the tissue under her chin to protect her little lace collar, "but she thought Dad might feel lonely if he had to go back and sit by himself. Gwenn wouldn't be any help to him; and anyway, Jen always does give up for someone else. Gwenn said she didn't have a decent wedding of her own, so she was *determined* to be in this one."

"She'll be pretty."

Tippy took her frail pink dress from its hanger on a wall light and slipped it over her head. The three attendants' gowns shaded from the faint shell pink of Christy Drayton's to Gwenn's deep rose; and from under a billowing froth, she said, "It was sweet of you to ask Theo for Bobby. She's staying in New York this week and I don't think he'd have come alone."

"Does he like her?"

"Sort of. He'll probably marry her if she'll wait around long enough for him—so she can keep him in the style to which he's planned to become accustomed."

The dress was in place, and she ran up the zipper and settled its folds as she asked, "Do you realize that this is the last time we'll ever talk this way? You'll be *married*. You'll be Alice Jordon Drayton."

"I'll still be Alcie. Just because I'll have a home of my own won't make any difference."

"Yes, it will." Tippy walked slowly to the dresser and leaned on it. "I'm not going to break down, or anything," she said, "because I've ordered myself not to. But there will be a difference. A lot bigger one than if—if Ken were coming back. We'd still be planning together, just as we did for a little while last fall. I'd be interested in a house, too, and taking notes from yours."

"But you'll still come down to Bucks County, won't you?" Alice urged. "Peter has a whole month, and you'll let him bring you down, won't you? I want you to be my very first guest. Promise?"

"I'll try to, Alcie. If I get through this wedding in a blaze of glory, I'll try. We mustn't let ourselves grow too far apart."

"We never could. If only. . . ." Alice stopped and bit her carefully reddened lips. This was no time to suggest changing friendship to sisterhood; so she only said, "If you'll come as soon as we come home from Canada, Tip, I'd make this about the fastest wedding trip a bride ever took. Please say you will."

"I might. Want me to round up the others now?"

"Is it time?"

"Almost. Now stand right where you are."

Tippy went to the door and opened it. She looked back at Alice who was leaning toward her own radiant face in the mirror. "Good-by, Alcie," she said softly, and closed the door behind her.

It was a beautiful wedding. Tippy stood in the receiving line and heard hundreds of people say how lovely the bride was, how sweet the old stone chapel had looked. She was glad the Officers Club had built on a new room for its receptions. She thought she couldn't have borne it to stand in the old lounge where she had received her guests on her sixteenth birthday. This big, new room held no memories. There was nothing in it to remind her of the nervous fright she had had every time Ken passed by, or the excitement she had felt when he asked her to dance. It had been such sweet misery to follow his steps.

Penny didn't come. Her mother and father did, and Bobby and Theo. Tippy stayed close to them while Alice cut her wedding cake; and when the bride's bouquet came sailing at her, she stepped back and let Jon's sister catch it. But she threw rice with abandon, and ran along with Peter behind the car. She even jerked off her satin slipper and sent it sailing, hopping along on one foot while Peter retrieved it.

"You'd have felt fine if it had gone off on a fender," he said, stooping to slip it on again.

But she only answered, "I like you in blues. You're very handsome, did you know it?"

"Me?" He made a face and linked their arms together. "I'm no beauty," he declared, "so don't try to kid me. I'm neat and tidy, but I've never been mobbed for my looks."

"*I* think you're handsome." Tippy stood still and said, "Perhaps it's like Penny says about Josh: You're more handsome *inside* than out. I think you're the handsomest man I know."

"Please don't ever change." He started her back to the

club and said hoarsely, "Don't ever change, Tip. I'll try to grow handsomer for you every day."

It was hard to settle down after the week of the wedding. Tippy began to realize how much it and June Week had filled the empty days of her life. Hard as they had been in many ways, they had given her little time to think. Now there was nothing else to do.

"It *is* easier to keep busy," she told Bobby, who was quite content to lounge on the terrace, in an old shirt and slacks. "I thought you were going to hunt a job."

"Plenty of time. I thought you were."

"Plenty of time."

He was comfortably stretched out in an old swing that had seen good army service, with a glass of lemonade on the stones beside him, a peach, a plate of Trudy's cookies, and a book propped on his chest.

"Don't you ever fill up?" she asked.

"Not often enough."

He groped for whatever connected first with his hand, and she pushed his feet aside and sat down. "Bobby," she asked wistfully, "would you drive me somewhere?"

"Sure. Where do you want to go?"

"I don't know."

"Over to Pen's maybe? We might take a look at Gladstone and see if it's being kept up all right for David and Carrol. Want to do that?"

"No. I don't know what I want to do."

He was in the middle of a good mystery story but he laid it face down under his chin and looked at her over it. She had seemed to be his special problem all this last week and had tagged around after him in a very complimentary way. Once he would have sent her off and said, "Stay lost," but now he couldn't. She was so much thinner than she should have been; and he picked up a cookie from his plate and offered it to her. "Have one?" But she shook her head, so he ate it himself. "I tell you what," he said while she watched him, "if you'll pay for the tickets, I'll drive you over to the summer stock company. I'll even blow you to dinner if you have enough dough."

"I'll see how much is left from my allowance."

No one ever got something for nothing, from Bobby. During the following week Tippy paid for a number of entertaining evenings he thought up, and they had fun together. He took her with him when she knew he preferred to go alone or with another girl, and they rode along and talked the way she had always hoped they would. It was mostly of their childhood and what he wanted to do with his future. They rarely spoke of Ken, and of Peter only once. That was the night they went to New York and he met a girl he knew.

"Betsy asked me to her dance," he grumbled when they left the restaurant. "I'd like to go. I mean stag, and not with you. Isn't Peter ever coming home?"

"You know he had to go on a fishing trip with his father," she explained patiently, sensing how he felt and secretly a little amused by his frank way of disposing of her. "He couldn't help it. After all, he owes his father something."

She gave him a sidewise glance which he took as a personal insult, for he stalked along and retorted grumpily, "Meaning I don't do anything for Dad. I'd like to know what he'd want to do with *me*."

"Oh, Bobby, you're such a funny dope." Tippy enjoyed him. She was older now than he, much older; and she told him, as Penny might have done, "You don't have to take me to the dance. I wouldn't want to go."

"But I can't leave you sitting at home," he protested. "I'd worry. I wouldn't have any fun."

"Peter should be back before then, or maybe—well, I may go down to Alcie's."

She had no intention of going off on a visit, but he caught the straw like a drowning man. "Say, that's swell," he said with relief. "I'll drive you down tomorrow, huh?"

"You'll drive me nowhere except home. Who ever heard of dropping in on a bride the very first week she's trying to settle a new house?"

"Alcie doesn't settle houses," he returned. "She just looks at 'em and everything hops into place."

Tippy wished she hadn't spoken. He hounded her. He even hopped out of bed unusually early the next morning to remind her of the telephone call she had promised to make. "I *didn't promise*, Bobby," she argued. "I only mentioned it."

But he had the telephone number written on a piece of paper and offered to put in the call. "I asked the operator for it," he explained into her grim but astonished stare. "Want me to ring?"

"I most certainly do not." And she marched down the stairs and out to the kitchen.

"He's only tryin', honey," Trudy said, when Tippy had sputtered out the story with indignant gestures. "He come out here early and says, 'Trudy, coax her to go. Poor kid, she ought to.' And your mama kind of thinks so, too, and

so does your papa. They's been aworryin' terrible about
you, and was wishin' we could all go off on a trip—maybe
out to Mr. David's, at Fort Knox."

"I'd rather go to Alcie's."

"You wouldn't have to stay but a night or two," Trudy
pointed out. "Jus' for a little change."

"Change?" Tippy sat down at the table and put her face
in her hands. "Why must I always be running around for
a *change?*" she cried. "I don't need it. I don't need anything, except. . . ." She swallowed and slid her hands
down to cover her chin and hide its quiver. "I can't spend
my whole life running," she said.

"You ain't agoin' to, child." Trudy left the toast she was
making and stood beside the table, smoothing Tippy's
curls. "Happiness is comin' to you," she said, "just as sure
as a rainbow comes in the sky after a rain. It may not be
the same rainbow you was seekin' for, but it's goin' to be
bright an' shinin'. It takes time, child, to start seein' what's
behind the clouds again. Sorrow sort of dims our eyes.
You want your breakfast now?"

Tippy tried to eat. The bacon was crisply fluted, just
the way she liked it, but she fed it to Switzy. She gave him
her toast, too, and drank only the strong, hot coffee.
Bobby, she had no doubt, was comfortably absorbed in
one of his interminable mysteries, so she went outside and
wandered down to the little brook.

It was cool and peaceful there. Switzy snuffled through
the grass and risked wet feet to retrieve the sticks she
tossed into the shallow water. A robin perched on a limb
and scolded. Should she go to Alcie's? she worried. I
wouldn't want her to visit me so soon, she thought, snap-

ping a twig and tossing half of it. I wouldn't want her if Ken and I were just starting housekeeping. If the Jordons had given us lovely silver candelabra like the ones we gave Alcie, I'd want to set the table just for the two of us and use all my new china and glass. I wouldn't want another girl sitting around. Or would I?

She considered the matter gravely. "I'd want Alcie," she decided aloud, lying back with her hands clasped under her head. "Yes, I'd want Alcie. I'd know Ken would be coming home in the evening, and I'd want to share my happiness with her. Yes, I'd want her very much, if I thought she was sad and lonely."

She heard voices and sat up to look toward the house. Peter's new green car stood in the driveway and General Jordon's boom reached all the way to the brook.

"We just stopped by on our way home," he shouted. "Couldn't hold this boy of mine any longer, so we brought you a basket of fish packed in ice."

The whole family was at the car, and even Switzy went. Tippy knew she should follow, too, but she saw Peter watch the bounding black ball and look past him. Then he waved. Switzy reversed himself, and the two of them came down the gentle slope.

"Hi," Peter said, dropping down beside her. "I never did care much for fishing."

"You stayed long enough." The words popped out through her loneliness, and she laughed because she sounded like a wife whose husband had stayed out too long of an evening. "I meant that I missed you," she said.

"Sure 'nuff?" Peter drew up his knees and clasped his arms around an old pair of cadet trousers. "Heck, did I miss you!" he returned with great feeling. "Have you ever camped in the woods with the stars so close you could reach up and touch them, and the wind making little sighing sounds through the trees? Believe me, it's wasted beauty—if you're there with your father. It's lonesome. But if you're with a girl—*the* girl—oh, man, it could be Heaven. Especially if she likes to fish. Do you?"

"I've never tried it."

"You ought to learn. When I get me a wife," he said, "she's going to learn." He turned his head and grinned at her. "I don't suppose I should marry a very fancy kind of wife, do you? I mean the always-in-the-beauty-shop kind?"

"Like Maxsie?"

"Yep, like Maxsie," he answered, knowing she was teasing him, but pretending to consider the matter. "My wife ought to be able to climb around over rocks, and stand in the water, and not be afraid of bugs. There's a bug on you," he said.

Tippy jumped. "Where?" she asked, and he leaned over to brush it off.

"It's just a firefly—suffering from insomnia and awake in the daytime. No, Maxsie wouldn't be my kind of a wife."

"Who would be, Peter?" Tippy leaned over to ask. "What kind of a wife would you really want?"

"Well, let me see." He looked up through the tree branches and thought for a moment. "I guess I'd want a —pal," he said carefully, searching for any words Ken might not have used and for any part of Tippy Ken might not have needed. "I'd want someone who would make me feel important and build me up. She wouldn't have to be an army girl," he said with strange insight, "because I know the ropes. I'd like for her to be, though. I'd be proud to have the army strain on both sides."

"Would you want children?"

"Yeah, I guess so. We've had such stacks of them in our family that I guess I could bear it if they didn't come along too soon. I never did have a chance to be the baby," he said with a grin, "so I'd rather have my wife just fuss over me for a while."

Poor Peter. Tippy looked at him and realized that no one in the whole Jordon family had ever had much time to wonder if the oldest boy were happy or not. He had had girls above and below him, and it was a brother's duty to look after the girls. "Poor Peter," she said aloud.

"Poor Peter, nothing," he shot back. "Why, I've had good training. I'll make a swell husband. There's nothing I don't know about putting on galoshes, or picking up around a house. I can close my eyes to cold cream and pinned-up hair—I don't even see 'em any more—and I can cram all my stuff into one drawer, and give up my turn at the car without crabbing. Some girl's going to get a prize. Would you be brave enough to try me, Tippy?"

The smiling game was gone from his eyes. They were a sober gray as they looked into hers, and his next words were deep with meaning. "I'm not Ken," he said. "I'm nothing like him; not in looks or disposition. Maybe that's good. I wouldn't always be reminding you of him by the things I said or the way I acted. I'm such a different kind of guy. But I love you, Tippy. I'd do my level best to make you happy."

"Oh, Peter." She wanted to say more but his words rushed on.

"You aren't the kind of girl to take a job," he told her. "You aren't even the kind to live alone. You're made for marriage, and to make a husband feel as if he's king of the world. I'd bring Ken back for you if I could, you know that. I'd trade places with him—but I can't. Don't you see that, Tip? I can only offer you a second-best love."

"Yes. Yes, I see it, Peter. I want your love. It isn't a second-best kind, though. It's a *wonderful* love. I do want it, but. . . . Oh, Peter."

She put her hands over her face but he pulled them gently away. "Don't, darling," he said. "You mustn't cry."

Ken had written that. Peter said it now; her mother, father, Bobby, Trudy. The whole world told her not to cry. "Smile and forget," they said. "Smile up your face." Tippy drew in a shuddering breath, and Peter put his arm around her.

"Don't, darling," he said. "I didn't mean to rush you. We just got to kidding and it all slipped out. It doesn't matter."

"But I want you happy, Peter," she said wistfully. "I love you differently from the way I loved Ken, but I truly love you. I do so want to make you happy."

She took his hand and held it in both of hers. She held it tightly, as if it were something dear to keep. "Oh, Peter, dear," she sighed, "be patient with me. Don't say any more, just be patient." And she sat with her eyes on the trees across the little brook. Off beyond them were the hills; the far, far hills that rolled away in the distance. There, so Ken had said, the little Man of the Mountain looked down on all the stupid human beings who try to destroy what God has made.

Peter's hand was warm in hers, warm and tender; and only her heart wept in the silence.